The Urbana Free Library

To renew: call 217-367-4057
or go to *"urbanafreelibrary.org"*
and select "Renew/Request Items"

THE DEVIL IN THE VALLEY

The Devil in the Valley

A NOVEL

Castle Freeman, Jr.

OVERLOOK DUCKWORTH
NEW YORK • LONDON

This edition first published in hardcover in the United States and the United Kingdom in 2015 by Overlook Duckworth, Peter Mayer Publishers, Inc.

NEW YORK
141 Wooster Street
New York, NY 10012
www.overlookpress.com
For bulk and special sales, please contact sales@overlookny.com,
or write us at the above address

LONDON
30 Calvin Street
London E1 6NW
info@duckworth-publishers.co.uk
www.ducknet.co.uk

Library of Congress Cataloging-in-Publication Data

Freeman, Castle, 1944-
The devil in the valley / Castle Freeman, Jr. — First edition.
pages ; cm   I. Title.
PS3556.R3838D48 2015   813'.54--dc23   2015024439

Book design and typeformatting by Bernard Schleifer
Manufactured in the United States of America
ISBN US: 978-1-4683-1217-1
ISBN UK: 978-0-7156-5052-3

FIRST EDITION
2 4 6 8 10 9 7 5 3 1

For Stona Fitch

But thinkest thou heaven is such a glorious thing?
I tell thee, Faustus, it is not half so fair
As thou, or any man that breathes on earth.

—CHRISTOPHER MARLOWE,
   *The Tragical History of the Life
          and Death of Doctor Faustus* (1604)
   Act II, Scene 2

CONTENTS

THE DEVIL IN THE VALLEY

PROLOGUE
THE CLOSER AND THE COP

OOKING RIGHT ALONG, WITH THE TOP DOWN AND THE breeze whistling past his hairy, slightly pointed ears, on a fresh new mission, feeling fit and frisky in the warm early-spring afternoon, Dangerfield, the account man, the closer, motored into the valley at the wheel of his beloved MGA, a classic like its driver. Spinning through the curves of the little two-lane, admiring the blooming trees, the blooming shrubs, the blooming daffodils or whatever the hell they were by the roadside, he at first missed the cruiser in his rearview, its blue light going.

Damnation, said Dangerfield. He pulled over.

Dangerfield watched the cop car in his side mirror. Then he smiled. For there emerged from the cruiser not the massive, bull-necked, buzz-cut colossus of his expectation, but a slender young woman who looked to carry no more than a hundred pounds, most of it in the equipment belt which, on leaving the cruiser, she settled atop her narrow hips. She placed a flat-brim state trooper hat on her head, leveled it, and approached the MGA. Dangerfield waited. This was going to be fun.

Is there a problem, officer? asked Dangerfield when the young woman stood at his window.

"No, sir," said the cop, "but there soon will be. You're about to run out of road. Pavement ends right up here around the bend. After that, it's pretty soft for a mile or so, pretty muddy. I saw you heading for it. I thought I'd warn you. A friendly warning."

Thanks, Sweetheart, said Dangerfield. *I'm not worried about a little mud.*

"You should be, sir. You'll never make it in this." The young officer glanced dubiously over the MGA.

I'll make it. I always get where I'm going.

The young officer gave him an appraising look. Did she sense something not right about this stop, something off?

"Where are you going, sir?" she asked.

Taft. I'm looking for a Mr. Taft. You know him?

"No, sir, but I know his place. He's up here past the unpaved section. Like I said, you won't make it this way. You might go around the other way."

Sure, sure, said Dangerfield. He smiled at her. *Tell me, Sweetheart,* he said, *are you really a cop?*

"Trooper Madison, sir. Brattleboro Barracks. Vermont State Police."

Reason I ask, said Dangerfield. *For a second, there, I thought maybe you were a Girl Scout.*

The trooper's eyes narrowed. "Sir?"

But then, Dangerfield went on, *I guess the Girl Scouts aren't issued three-fifty-sevens, even in Vermont. Or are they?* He smiled again, blandly, and nodded at the revolver mounted on the young trooper's heavy belt.

The trooper didn't smile.

"May I see your license and registration, sir?"

Dangerfield feigned surprise. *Absolutely, officer, but why? I thought this was a friendly warning.*

"License and registration, sir, please."

Dangerfield handed them over. The trooper examined them.

"What kind of a license is this, sir?"

Special permit.

"Wait here, please, sir," the trooper said. "I'll have to run this."

Mind if I stretch while you do that? said Dangerfield, and made to open his door.

"Remain seated, please, sir. Do not exit your vehicle." Dangerfield sat back. Now for the fun.

The trooper returned to her cruiser. She removed her hat and slipped into the driver's seat. She bent to her radio. Suddenly, the man in the little car looked to her like all kinds of wrong, all kinds of bad news. She would run his license, if it was a license; and, though she hated to do so, she would call for assistance. She keyed her radio. She looked up and toward the sports car to get a plate number. She looked again.

The MGA was gone. The driver was gone. He hadn't driven off. He and his vehicle had disappeared. The road was empty. Where the car had been, beside the road, was nothing but the budding woodland and the nodding daffodils. Dangerfield had vanished.

BACKPACKER IN THE DARK WOOD

MATERIAL, SAID TAFT, CONTENT, PLOT. WHERE'S THE PLOT? Need a plot. Not doing well. Could be doing better. In a bit of a spot, here, no question. Why? What lacks? Have health, friends (well, one friend), enough money, a place, the right place—a home. And yet, feeling checked, feeling stuck, hung up, as though the train's come to a halt but hasn't arrived. There's no station, there are no people. Out the window and all around, cinders and dry weeds and trash: food wrappers, old tires, busted supermarket carts, plastic bags blowing. Waste ground. That feeling. What is that? Age? Sounds like it. Age, and, thus, nothing new: just another backpacker in the Dark Wood. Got off the trail. Got lost. Old story . . .

Bored.

. . . Old story. Needed? A path, a push—What's that?

I said, bored. Bored, bored, bored.

Taft jumped. "What?" he asked. "Who?"

Bored. You're bored, Chief. You're boring yourself to death.

"Who's there?"

Over here.

Taft turned. Dangerfield was sitting in the rocking chair on the porch to his left. Dangerfield was enjoying the old rocker. Back and forth, back and forth went Dangerfield. Pleased with the simplest things. A big kid he was, really, in some ways.

"Who are you?" Taft asked.

I'm your pal. I'm your sidekick. I'm the guide at your side.

"Guide to what?"

To whatever you need. To everything.

"I don't need a guide," said Taft.

It appears you do, though, Chief. Am I right, or am I right? You just said it. You're lost. Therefore, you need a guide. In any case, here I am.

"Uh-huh," said Taft. "Alright, okay. What are you selling?"

I'm not selling anything, Chief. I'm buying. You're selling.

"Hah. Not likely. How did you get here?"

It wasn't easy, said Dangerfield. *Would you believe, I almost got busted by some female baby cop, some Campfire Girl of a state trooper? I told her, I heard this was pretty wild country, but I didn't know the Girl Scouts carried three-fifty-sevens. Pretty good, I thought: Girl Scouts? Three-fifty-sevens? Hah. She didn't laugh. Silly bitch. What the hell is that? Is that your idea of law enforcement up here?*

"I don't know what you're talking about," said Taft. "What trooper?"

Don't have much to do with the police, I guess?

"No."

No wonder you're bored. My advice? Transgress.

"Not my style."

Take a cruise.

"Not interested in cruises."

Ever been on a cruise?

"No."

Come on, Chief. How do you know you're not interested, then?

"Come on, yourself," said Taft. "You don't have to have had a thing to know you don't want it. Have you ever had the plague?"

Quite a few times. It's not too bad when you're used to it.

Taft looked at him. A stout man, around Taft's own age, prosperous, sleek, well-barbered, his dark, graying hair combed straight back and worn full behind, his beard neatly trimmed. A bit of a dude as well, turned out in dapper suburban gentleman's motoring outfit: houndstooth-check jacket, blue oxford shirt, good cord trousers, kid leather driving gloves, cloth cap. Dangerfield rocked his chair gently, his gaze moving to take in the surround: Taft's porch, his side yard, the road, the woods across the road, the distant hills, green, then blue, then gray, then gone in the distance.

No wonder you're bored, Dangerfield said at last. *This place is five miles the other side of nowhere. What do you do up here for fun?*

"The same things everybody else does," said Taft. "The same things you do."

I doubt that, Chief.

"What do you want?" Taft asked him.

I don't want anything. You do. You want to feel better. You want to not be stuck. You want to not be bored. You want to get off of that train. You want action. You said it yourself: plot. You want a plot. I can get you a plot. I can get you a hell of a plot. I've got a deal for you, Chief.

"What deal?"

It's pretty simple, really, said Dangerfield. Then he stopped. He looked to his right, past Taft's shoulder. Suddenly alert, he dropped his voice. *Who's this?* He whispered.

Eli Adams came around the corner of the house. He had been at Taft's putting new glass in a broken window upstairs. "You're all set," said Eli. "Who's here? Was somebody here?"

Tell him nobody, whispered Dangerfield.

"Nobody," said Taft.

Eli looked at the rocking chair, creaking gently to and fro. "What's the matter with your chair?" he asked.

The wind, murmured Dangerfield. *Tell him it's the wind.*

"Nothing's the matter with it," said Taft. "The wind's moving it. Feel the draft?"

"Who were you talking to?" Eli asked him. "I thought I heard you talking to somebody."

"Myself."

"Oh," said Eli. "Oh, okay. Listen: you want me to, someday, I can get a ladder to that big tree around there and trim that branch so it won't hit the window when it blows. That's your trouble, right there."

"Someday," said Taft. "How much do I owe you for today?"

"I don't know," said Eli. "I'll put it on your tab."

"Sure, you will," said Taft.

Eli gave the rocking chair a last look. "Well, I'm due at Marcia's," he said.

"Marcia, yes," said Taft. "How's Billy?"

"Sean. Kid's name's Sean. He's not good. Not good at all."

"I'm sorry," said Taft.

Eli turned and started back around the house where his truck was parked. "Okay," he said.

"We'll see you," Taft called after him.

Who was that? asked Dangerfield when Eli had gone.

"Oh, that's Eli," said Taft. "Lives on the next hill. He helps out with things. He's handy. I'm not. He's a friend."

Asks a lot of questions, doesn't he?

"I don't know. Does he?"

Watch out for him, said Dangerfield. *Be careful. That was good, though, just now. The draft? Talking to yourself? That was very good. That works. You catch on fast, Chief.*

"Eli couldn't see you, could he?" asked Taft.

No. He couldn't see me.

"Can anybody see you?"

You can.

"Anybody else?"

Nobody you know, Chief, said Dangerfield.

"Ah," said Taft.

So, that's how we work it, see? Dangerfield went on. *That's how we work our deal. It's a partnership. I'm the silent partner. Very, very silent. We keep it close. We keep it dark. You and I? We're together. I'm with you, you're with me. We're clear. Everybody else, no. If you're with me, you're alone for everybody else. Get it?*

"Not so fast," said Taft. "What do you mean, 'That's how we work our deal'? We don't have anything to work. We don't have a deal."

Don't we, Chief?

"No."

What's the problem?

"What's the problem? Well, for one thing, I don't believe you. Not a word. Okay? You're full of holes, you are. For example, you said a state trooper pulled you over on your way here, right?"

That's right. So?

"How, though?" Taft demanded. "You're invisible. But the trooper saw you?"

She thought she did. Then she didn't.

"What's that mean?"

Look, Chief, said Dangerfield. *It's got to do with the Talents, okay?*

"What talents?"

Dangerfield was impatient. He waved his hand dismissively. *Gifts*, he said, *abilities, tools. Powers. Talents. You don't need to get way off into the high grass about the Talents. The Talents are my department. Let me worry about them. Suffice to say: they're impressive. They're what you need, Chief. I have them. I give them to you. Well, I lend them to you. You use them. They're fun. Have fun with them.*

"Fun?"

All kinds of fun, said Dangerfield. *That plot you're looking for? The Talents are the plot. They're the plot's front end. They're something, Chief. You'll see. But remember: be careful. If you're talking to me, you're talking to nobody. Don't forget that. Your neighbors, that guy that just left—they'll think you're nuts if you're not careful.*

"They think that as it is," said Taft. He looked narrowly at Dangerfield. "Maybe they're right," he said. "Maybe, at last, they're right. Maybe that's what this is."

Meaning maybe you've gone around the bend? said Dangerfield. *Wrong. You're not nuts. You were, maybe, or on the way. You're not any more. It's all real.*

"It's all real," said Taft.

What do you think, Chief? That's my deal. How do you like it?

"How do I like it? How do I know? All I see so far is about you. Your being here or not being here. Your so-called Talents. Everybody's got talents, don't they? What are yours? Can you play the ukulele? Can you wiggle your ears? Can you fly? So what? What's that do for me? What's your deal, for me? What can I have?"

That's not the question, Chief. The question is, what do you want?

"Ah," said Taft.

Beginning to get it now, are you?

Taft was silent.

Chief? Dangerfield pressed him. But Taft wasn't ready.

"Why should I believe you're what you say you are?" he asked.

What do I say I am, Chief?

"You know as well as I do," said Taft. "Don't fence with me. Tell me how I know you can do what you say you can."

Try me.

Taft thought for a moment. Then he smiled. He turned to Dangerfield. "Alright," he said. "Something I need? Something I would really like? New tires for the truck. It will never pass inspection this year. Four new tires. What about it?"

Come on, Chief, said Dangerfield. *Spread your wings a little, here. All the kingdoms of the world, and the glory of them, I offer you. Riches beyond the dreams of avarice I offer you. And you go for new rubber?*

"I don't need all the kingdoms of the world, and the rest of it," said Taft. "I do need tires. This is a test, right? I hear you mocking me, I hear you talking large, I hear you quoting fancy verse, but I don't see you making anything happen. Can you?"

Go look.

Taft left the porch and went to the barn where he kept his truck. In a couple of minutes, he was back.

"I asked you for four new tires," he told Dangerfield. "That's not four new tires. That's a whole new truck."

Happy birthday, Chief.

"You didn't get me what I asked for, though, did you?"

Dangerfield sighed. *Am I going to have trouble with you, Chief?* he asked. *Alright. Okay. Suit yourself. You've got your old wreck back, new treads all around. You want to go see?*

"No."

Go ahead. Don't take my word. Check it out. See for yourself.

"No need."

Then you believe I can do what I say I can?

"Yes."

You ready to do business, then?

"Maybe."

No maybe, Chief. Yes or no.

"Come on," said Taft. "What do you take me for? We still don't have a deal, do we? Not yet. We have half a deal. I get whatever I want. You give me your famous Talents. I use them. That's your part. I still don't know what my part is."

I think you do, Chief. I think you know damned full well.

Taft took a moment. He nodded. Then he said, "It's like a contract, right?"

It's not like a contract. It is a contract. Oh, boy, is it a contract.

"And when it's up, then you come for me and I have to go with you?"

Right.

"And until then, you fetch me what I ask for. What I want, you supply, whatever it is, you get it. You serve me."

Absolutely.

"And that contract, our contract?" Taft went on, "for your service? It runs for how long? Twenty-some years, I think, right?"

Where do you get that idea?

"My reading," said Taft.

Dangerfield rocked right back in his chair, with a whoop of laughter. Pitching forward, he slapped his knees.

Oh, Chiefy, Chiefy, he laughed. *Your what? Your reading? You old English Major, you! What is it you're giving me, here? You're giving me Christopher Marlowe, aren't you? 'Four and twenty years being expired, the articles above written inviolate, etcetera, etcetera, grant full power to carry, etcetera, body and soul, flesh, blood, and goods into their habitation wheresoever.' Hah. You crack me up, Chief.*

"What's so funny?"

You are. You're living in the Middle Ages. Your friend Marlowe's been dead for four hundred years, and between ourselves he didn't have a lot on the ball when he walked among us. Second- or third-chop poet? Some kind of a half-assed spy? Killed in a bar fight? What an adolescent! In fact, he's mainly spread a lot of misinformation and done a lot of harm. The world has changed, you know. It moves a little faster than it did when Good Queen Bess was in the chair. We're not mortgage bankers, Chief. We're strictly short-term. Think of us as payday lenders.

"How long, then?" Taft asked him.

I can get you six months.

"Six months?"

I might be able to stretch it to seven, said Dangerfield. *I'll have to see. I don't write the contracts, you know.*

"Who does?"

The Legal Department, of course. Plus, the big man. The CEO. My boss. My superior. I have to get him to sign off for anything over six months. I can probably get you the seven, though. The big man's got a soft heart. He shouldn't have one, but he does.

"Seven months," said Taft. "Til October."

We'll say Columbus Day. It's a good contract, Chief. It means you won't have to miss the foliage.

But even now Taft wasn't quite there. He looked at Dangerfield. "What I don't understand," he said, "is you. How is it you're here at all? I didn't ask for you."

Didn't you, Chief? What about plot—and its lack? What about feeling stuck? What about that train, that Dark Wood? You cried out, Chief. We heard you.

"We?"

My firm.

"You mean there are more of you?"

Oh, absolutely. We're a major firm. We're big. Resources? We've got them. As for your own situation? Dangerfield shrugged. *We know these things. It's what we do.*

"But how?" asked Taft.

We mark the sparrow's fall, Chief.

"Alright, but why the secrecy?" Taft asked him. "If I'm with you, I'm alone. If I'm talking to you, I'm talking to myself. Nobody's to know anything about you, about our . . . arrangement. Everybody's in the dark. Eli, everybody. Why?"

Standards, Chief. Quality control. Listen, if people knew about the deal you're going to make—the upside, the Talents, the rest—the whole world would be breaking down our door. We'd be swamped. Service would suffer. We need to keep out the riffraff.

"What if I tell?" Taft asked.

Be a mistake. A very big mistake. Telling voids the deal. We wouldn't have a choice, then. We'd have to cut right to the downside. Not a good outcome, especially for you. Bad idea, Chief. Don't even think of it.

Taft nodded. "Okay," he said.

So? said Dangerfield. *Here we are, right? Time to jump, Chief. What do you say? In or out. Up or down. Right here. Right now.*

Taft nodded again. He swallowed. He scratched his head. He looked out over the dooryard. Then he clapped his hands lightly together.

"Done deal," he said.

Attaboy, Chief. You won't regret it.

"Seven months," said Taft. "Columbus Day. Then you come for me, yes? You take me anyplace you want?"

Not any place, Chief. One place.

Taft smiled. "The hot place," he said.

Hot enough.

"I'm not worried about that, though," said Taft. "I worked in Philadelphia for a couple of years. August in Philadelphia? I don't mind heat."

Well, it's not the heat so much, said Dangerfield. *It's the time. We're talking Eternity, here, Chief.*

"Not worried about that, either. I can last it. We're in Vermont, remember? For us, Eternity is another name for March."

I like your spirit, Chief.

"Where do I sign?"

Oh, you've already signed. You signed a few minutes ago, when you lied to your friend.

"Ah," said Taft.

You wouldn't have a drink in the house? Dangerfield asked him.

"Got a bottle of Sir Walter's."

What's that?

"Scotch whiskey."

Never heard of it, said Dangerfield.

"It's a small label," said Taft. "You might call it sub-premium."

Perfect. What do you say, Chief? Shall we have a drink to our partnership?

"A drink?" said Taft. "I'm your man."

Not yet, but you will be.

"Come with me," said Taft. He got to his feet.

After you, Chief, said Dangerfield, and he let Taft go before him into the house.

2

HAPPY THE MAN WHOSE FATHER GOES TO THE DEVIL

THOSE HAVING BUSINESS WITH LANGDON TAFT TRIED TO get to him by eleven in the morning. For Taft, the clear, bright hours were his best. He felt his momentum build from waking to about eleven. Eleven was when momentum slowed and distraction set in. Distraction, diversion—or the need of them. Or of their substitutes. One substitute in particular. Eleven was when Taft was known to pour his first dram of Sir Walter Scott. An ex-gentleman, ex-teacher, ex-scholar, ex-householder, ex-abstainer, he was retired from many things, indeed from most everything, but not, his friends and neighbors observed, from Sir Walter Scott.

In fact it was a slander. Taft was not a forenoon drinker. If he was found to be imbibing in the morning, it was not from habit, but because he had forgotten to leave off the night before. So it was, no doubt, on this day, at ten-thirty, when Eli Adams knocked on the door of the room Taft used for a study. Too late.

"Eli!" cried Taft. "Eli, old sport. Come you in. Sit you down. Have an eye-opener with us."

Be careful, whispered Dangerfield. He stood in the shadow behind Taft. Mysteriously, he was attired in a fresh, well-pressed, white lab coat over a crisp blue shirt and a red polka-dot bow tie. A stethoscope hung around his neck, and the left breast pocket of his lab coat was embroidered: MASSACHUSETTS GENERAL HOSPITAL. He might have been a prosperous surgeon. *Be careful*, he murmured.

"Us?" Eli asked.

Taft pushed the Sir Walter's across the desk toward Eli, pushed a glass after it. "Water?" he asked.

"Nothing, thanks. Nothing at all. Well, maybe some coffee?"

"No coffee," said Taft. "Don't use it. Don't keep it in the house. That stuff is bad for you, Eli. Bad. Doctor told me once if he could get his patients to do one thing? For their health? Cut out coffee. That's right, coffee. Worse than booze, worse than the cigs, worse than dope. Worse than loose women—"

"Worse than work?"

"Well, well," said Taft. "But you get my point. Coffee. Stay clear of coffee, Eli. Sit."

Eli took the chair across the desk from Taft.

Dangerfield bent to Taft's ear. *Ask him what he wants*, whispered Dangerfield.

"What can I do for you this morning, old man?" asked Taft.

"Went by Marcia's the other day after I left here," said Eli. "The little boy, you know."

"Bobby," said Taft.

"Sean. He's in Mass General. Been there a week."

"I don't like the sound of that."

"No," said Eli. "He has to have surgery before they can start treatments, I guess. They don't know what to do. Those big-shot doctors, all they get from them is the run-around. Carl hasn't been working full-time. Marcia cleans, when she can, but she has the baby, too."

Taft nodded. He raised his glass and took a sip. "Sure you won't—uh—," he said, pointing at the bottle.

Eli shook his head. "So I told her I'd come see you," he finished. "She said I wasn't to."

Dangerfield bent to Taft's ear again. Behind his hand he said softly, *Ask him what he thinks you can do. Are you a doctor?*

"I'm sorry for this," Taft told Eli. "But what is it you think I can do? Am I a doctor?"

"You know what you are," Eli told him. "You're a friend. An old friend. They've got the Mass General bills in a stack on top of the TV. Stack's two inches thick, and they've barely started. They're looking at tens, more likely hundreds of thousands or they lose their kid. Probably lose him anyway, in the end. They know that. They need help. You're able to help. Well able. And you're a friend of the family."

Not that family, tell him.

"Not that family," said Taft.

"Come on," said Eli.

"Come on, yourself, old fellow. You know the history."

"History, is right. What is it, thirty years?"

"We Tafts have long memories."

"So what?"

"So what? She threw me over, old sport."

"So what?" Eli asked again. "The little kid in Mass General didn't throw you over. His mother didn't throw you over. It was his grandmother did, for Christ's sake."

Behind Taft's chair, Dangerfield hissed. *I bet she wishes she hadn't, now*, he breathed to Taft.

"I bet she wishes she hadn't, now," said Taft.

"What was that?" asked Eli.

"I said, I bet—"

"I heard what you said. Okay, suit yourself. Marcia told me not to come. I'll be on my way," said Eli. But he kept his seat.

"She did?"

"Said I'd be wasting my time."

Taft smiled and shook his head. "But you knew better," he said.

"I thought I did."

"Relax, old sport," said Taft. "Come on, take the yardstick out of your rectum and have a boost with us, here." He pushed the Sir Walter's further toward Eli.

Careful.

"Us?" asked Eli.

"With me," said Taft. Eli poured two fingers of Sir Walter's into the glass and tasted it. He made a face.

"What's the matter?" Taft asked him.

"That's awful stuff," said Eli. "All the money you have, you can't get in a decent brand of Scotch? This tastes like ditch water."

"It's cheap," said Taft. "We Tafts are a saving people, you know. We're not Scots for nothing."

"Scots?"

"Lowland Scots. Like our friend." Taft nodded toward the bottle of Sir Walter's.

"I thought you were part of those Tafts that had the President Taft," said Eli.

"So we are—at a certain remove. And what were they? Border Scots, all of them."

"We're all Americans, I thought," said Eli.

"Don't go Ellis Island on me, here, old man. Point is, we're a provident people. That's why I'm able to help that poor little boy and his mother and his father and his perishing grandmother, God damn her black soul to hell."

Hear, hear, murmured Dangerfield.

"You will help them, then?" Eli asked him.

"What do you think?"

"Really help? The whole shot?"

"The whole shot," said Taft. "Do this, old boy: go back to Marcia. That two-inch stack of Mass General bills? Tell her to send it to me. Then in future, when more come, she's not even to open them. Just send them here."

"All of them?"

"All of them. She can forget about them. Her boy will be fine."

"I hope so."

"I know so."

Eli blinked. He laughed. "Well," he said. "Well, that's good, then. That's very good. I don't know what to say. Thank you. What made you change your mind?"

"I didn't change my mind, old sport. I just wanted to run you around a little. Forgive me."

"Nothing to forgive," said Eli. "I'll go to Marcia's right now. Well, I might have another drink before I go."

"Help yourself," said Taft.

"I might even buy you a bottle of something good."

"Don't bother, old boy. After about the first half a glass, quality doesn't matter much. He'll tell you the same," he turned his head slightly to glance up at Dangerfield.

"Who will?" asked Eli.

Careful, whispered Dangerfield.

● ● ●

When Eli Adams had left, Dangerfield slipped around Taft's desk and took the chair where the visitor had sat. He arranged his lab coat over his knees. He shook his head. *I told you and told you, Chief*, he said. *You need to be a little careful.*

"Careful?" Taft asked.

Discreet. You can't just bring me into the conversation. Not with outsiders. You know this.

"Eli's not an outsider."

Everybody's an outsider now, Chief. Remember that. Don't blow our deal because you have a couple of pops for breakfast and start loving your neighbor.

"Eli doesn't care about our deal. He's a friend."

Dream on, Chief. Friends? There are no friends. Never were. Never will be. There's only the deal. Remember that. But we won't argue. On the plus side, you played him very well. You had him going there for a minute, yes, you did. He thought you weren't going to unbelt for him.

"No," said Taft. "He knew I would. He knew from the start. He wouldn't have come if he hadn't known."

He looked like he didn't know. He said he didn't know.

"He was pretending."

Why would he do that?

"For fun," said Taft. "I told you: he's a friend."

Dangerfield shrugged. *If you say so, Chief. But why did you, anyway?*

"Why did I help them? Why would I not?" asked Taft. "They're my neighbors. They're good people."

What about the one who threw you over?

"Mollie? She's an old lady. She was something in her day. Our day. Really something. Big blue eyes. Big—you know. But now she looks like a dumptruck. You heard Eli. She's a grandmother."

She still threw you over, though, didn't she?

"It wasn't Mollie, it was her parents," said Taft. "Didn't approve of me. Can you believe it? Molly was willing. I think. Anyway, I don't hold a grudge."

The hell you don't, said Dangerfield. *And why not? If you've got a good grudge, don't waste it. Hold it. Hold it tight. My advice.*

But Taft shook his head. "Besides," he went on, "you heard him. The little boy's going to die."

So what do you care if he does?

"Very well. What would you do?"

Let him die. Look, he'll die someday, anyway. Not my problem. Not yours. Shit happens. Keep the money.

"Keep the money?"

Bingo, Chief.

"Keep the money, and do what with it?" Taft demanded. "What would you do? You won't help Marcia and Carl and Sean. You won't pay the doctors. What would you do?"

Oh, I don't know. Anything. Have fun. Travel. Not like you, anyway. All you do is sit here.

"What if I do? Did you really think when I signed on that I was going to go in for fancy cars, boats, houses? Race-horses? Sea cruises? Football teams?"

Why not?

"The trouble with you," Taft told Dangerfield, "is you've got no education. You've got no class."

Not like you, you mean. You're a regular aristocrat, aren't you? I wonder, though, Chief. I know something about aristocrats. I've done business with thousands of them. You don't look like one. You don't act like one. Your pal Eli thinks you're so rich. Are you?

Taft smiled. "Around here, if your tractor's paid off, you're rich," he said.

My point, Chief.

"To be sure, I'm luckier than most. I have a cushion."

A cushion, said Dangerfield. *Good thing, too, since I'm guessing you never were much of an earner. Am I right?*

"You're not wrong."

What about that cushion, then?

"Started with Grandad," said Taft. "Grandad wasn't a big man. Had a hardware store in the next town up the line here. Sold harness to farmers. But he was a careful man, a prudent man, and Dad was his only child. He meant that Dad should have opportunities. Dad went to the town academy, but then Grandad sent him to Harvard. He meant Dad should make useful friends. After that, he put him into a law office in Brattleboro. No law school. You learned the way you'd learn a trade, in an apprenticeship."

The way I learned, myself, said Dangerfield. *The best way.*

"I don't know. According to Dad, he never did learn much law. But he learned something almost as good."

Insurance? Banking?

"Real estate," said Taft. "Dad started investing. Nothing grand, just putting his spare change into properties. Raw land. Dad came along, you see, right after World War Two. This whole part of the country was in hard times. It was shut down. The doors were locked. The lights were out. The old-time, tit-squeezing dairy farmers had busted, the mills had busted. Nobody had a pot to piss in. You could have had the whole state for the price of a cut-rate cruise today."

How would you know, Chief? Dangerfield asked him. *You don't like cruises, remember? Cruises, boats, so on, they're for the likes of me, right? They're for peasants. Not you. You've got too much education, right? Too much class?*

"I'm sorry I said that. Whiskey talk. I must be a bit tight."

You're hammered, Chief. You're hammered, and it's not even noon. You might want to dial back on the sauce, don't you think?

"Hah," said Taft. "That's pretty rich, coming from you."

Friendly advice, Chief. But think it over. Where you're going, it can be hard to get a drink.

"Dry county, is it?"

Dry as dust. Dry as dry bones.

"I believe that, anyway," said Taft.

Go on with your story, Chief. Your father . . .

"Not much more to say. Turned out Dad hadn't exactly been buying all that land at random. He had those useful friends. Time the interstate highways began to get built into this country up here, lo and behold, Dad owned a good deal of the land they were built on—or, more to the point, he owned the land where they crossed. 'Mister Interchange,' they used to call him."

How did he know where they'd cross?

"He guessed."

Lucky, wasn't he? said Dangerfield. *You know, Chief? I'm going to have to remember to ask our IT Department to run your name in the archives. I'm thinking we might have more than one file.*

"You think?"

Oh, yes, said Dangerfield. *But either way, here you are. Your old man's lucky. You're lucky, too, aren't you?*

"Well," said Taft. "You know what they say?"

What do they say, Chief?

"Happy the man whose father goes to the devil."

Dangerfield showed a thin smile. *Put it that way,* he said.

"So, there you have it," said Taft. "My cushion."

That's it? asked Dangerfield. *That's the cushion? You could hardly get two cats' asses comfortable on a cushion that size, could you? It amounts to a shit-hook lawyer, not super-honest, who dabbles in real estate. That, and a few gas stations. Some cushion. It's small time, Chief. Cub Scout stuff. Not high value, not at all. So how about all those tens of thousands, hundreds of thousands you're going to send to Mass General for poor little what's-his-name? Can the cushion really front that, like you told Adams?*

"What do you think?"

Me? I don't know. How should I?

"I bet you do, though. I bet you know to the penny."

You lose. I'm not your accountant.

"What are you, then?"

I'm your spiritual advisor, said Dangerfield. *Come on, Chief. Be honest. Can the cushion really cover the kind of bills you say these people are looking at?*

"Not close," said Taft.

Well?

"That's where you come in, isn't it? Mass General bills Marcia. Marcia bills me. I bill you. Right?"

Absolutely. That's our contract.

"Another thing," said Taft.

What's that, Chief?

"It's more than the bills," said Taft. "Jimmy, the kid in Mass General? He gets better. Permanent remission. Complete recovery. Got that? He comes home. He's fine. A long and happy life for little Jimmy."

Whoa, Chief, said Dangerfield. *Slow down. I don't know. Our contract's for the money, here, not for medical miracles.*

"Whoa, yourself. Our contract is for whatever I say it's for."

I'm just telling you, said Dangerfield. *It's not something I can approve on my own. I'll have to take it to my superior.*

"We have a deal," said Taft. "Your superior can go to hell."

Dangerfield snickered. *Put it that way,* he said.

"Hah," said Taft. "Nor is he out of it, eh?"

Put it that way, Dangerfield said again. He grinned. *That's a pretty good line, Chief. Did you get that in your reading, too?*

"You bet," said Taft.

•   •   •

Thought Taft after Dangerfield's departure: fiends, writers, religious men, and educators—they always want to know about the money. Where is it? Who has it? Where did they get it? How much? Since when? Never was much interested, myself. Figured the poor you have always with you, likewise the rich. Use what you've got, not lavishly, but, especially for others, with the free, the open hand. No obligations, no game-playing. Give it out. Give it away. Secret of my unsuccess, no doubt.

Taft uncorked the Sir Walter's and poured himself a small one.

The free, the open hand, that's the ticket, whoever you are, whatever your line of work. Recall the good old story about Willie Sutton, the famous bank robber. Willie hits the Farmers' and Drovers' for a cool million, gets away clean. Then, the very next week, he hits the Merchants' and Traders', but there he's unlucky. Somebody ratted. The law's waiting for him. He gets caught. Cops have Willie down at the station house. They ask him, they say, "Willie, you just got a cool million from your last score, now here you are working again after only a week. What happened to the million you got from the Farmers' and Drovers'?" And Willie tells them, "Boys, it was like this. Yes, I walked out of the Farmers' and Drovers' with a cool million. But that was last week. Boys, she's all gone. Three hundred thousand I left at the track. Three hundred thousand I blew across the bar. Three hundred thousand I spent on the ladies of the night. And the last hundred thousand, I guess, I just kind of pissed away."

3

CALLIE AT THE DEPOT

THE VALLEY HOSPICE HAD A CORNER OF THE CLINIC'S upper floor: two cheerful bedrooms with a shared bath, and another room available as a sitting room for visitors, or, at need, as a third bedroom for—you might say—overflow. In those pleasant, plainly furnished quarters the Hospice workers, mainly volunteers, saw to the needs, to the comfort, if possible to the contentment, of their charges, men and women at the end of their lives and their friends and families. The theory of the Hospice was pretty simple: you went there to die, and perhaps, because nobody on the premises pretended otherwise, that corner of the building was a curiously ungloomy place. Some of the older people in the valley called it the Depot, the depot being where you went to catch the outbound train.

Calpurnia Lincoln had occupied one of the two ensuite Hospice rooms for a long enough time that her tenure had begun to be treated as a bit of a joke—not least by herself. "Still here," Calpurnia called to volunteers returned from two weeks' vacation. "Still ticking over. Still at the old stand." Calpurnia was ninety-eight. She couldn't walk very well, and she was a little deaf, but she was a good-humored old girl (at ninety-eight, you'd better be), and though herself without children, she was aunt, great-aunt, great-great-aunt, cousin, second cousin, third cousin to three quarters of the valley. What if she did linger rather long at the Hospice's feast? Who was going to put her out? She gave the place a good part of its tone. Besides, penniless, she had no place else to go.

Calpurnia was keen. She had all her marbles and quite possibly a few of yours. At the Hospice, she sometimes helped in the office with the paperwork. She wasn't a book reader, but she read the news, sometimes she watched the ballgame on her little TV, and she awaited visitors. She seldom waited long. Family and friends came and went. Having lived in the valley for a hundred years, close enough, and being perfectly lucid, Calpurnia was especially valuable to those having an interest in local history. She had been interrogated, annotated, commentated, celebrated, interviewed, photographed, recorded, reported, redacted, transcribed, filmed, videotaped—she'd all but been fixed in amber. She more than knew the history of their valley: she *was* that history. And if in some cases the remarkable detail of her recall had the truth of fiction, nevertheless it came from fact, or if it didn't, nobody living was in a position to say so.

Calpurnia Lincoln's most faithful visitor was Eli Adams. What the family relationship was between them was unclear to both, though in fact Calpurnia's grandfather's first wife had been Eli's mother's cousin. Not much of a connection, barely kinship at all, but sufficient. Decades earlier, when Calpurnia had worked at the post office, she had boarded with Eli's family on their farm. Eli was a young boy at that time. He and Calpurnia had become allies; she was his Aunt Callie. Now he dropped in to see her a couple of times a week. They bickered and bantered and batted things back and forth.

"Let me ask you something, okay?" said Eli. "You know Langdon Taft?"

Calpurnia sniffed. "That one," she said. "Your friend."

"Langdon. Is he, do you know, related to those Tafts from up the line, the ones who had the President Taft?"

"William Howard Taft," said Calpurnia.

"That's the one. Are Langdon's those same Tafts?"

"They wished they were, I'll bet," said Calpurnia. "William Howard Taft, you know, was—I don't even know—not only president. He was vice president, chief of the Supreme Court, secretary of war, probably more. He was a big fish, and I'm sure your friend Langdon (or his parents) would dearly love to call him a cousin. But I doubt they can."

"Why not?"

"You know as well as I do why not. Come on. Nobody would say your friend Langdon was built out of the kind of stuff that makes presidents and the rest, would they?"

"Wouldn't they?"

"They would not," said Calpurnia. "No, by the time the soup got passed down to Langdon's people, it was pretty thin, it looks like. After all, President Taft? His family bailed out of here after a generation or so, didn't they? Cleared out for Illinois or Ohio or someplace like that. Made their pile out there, not here. Your friend Langdon's people didn't have that kind of get-up-and-go. They sat tight. Still here. Never leave, except by way of the cemetery. That's what I meant about the soup."

"You've really got it in for poor Langdon today, don't you?"

"No, I don't," said Calpurnia. "I've hardly met the man. But some of what I've heard about him I wish I hadn't. Everybody knows he's a drinker. And worse. For example, Polly Jefferson, at the post office? Didn't she tell me just the other day they had a special delivery for Langdon Taft, and so she drove out there with it, went up to the house. Door was open partway, and Polly could hear your friend inside talking to somebody, just chatting away, some visitor. So, she called his name—'Mr. Taft?'—and he called out, sure, come on in. He was in his office, there, his study. He was in there, and he told Polly to come on in, so she did, and your friend was in there, alright, but he was all by himself. He was alone. Nobody was with him. He was in there talking to nobody, talking to himself."

"Probably talking on the phone, there, wasn't he?" asked Eli.

"Polly didn't think he was. She was pretty sure he wasn't on the phone, no."

"Well, what if he was talking to himself," asked Eli. "That makes him crazy?"

"It doesn't exactly make him regular, does it?" asked Calpurnia. "Now, I don't say he hasn't got his points, your friend. He knows how to make his manners. He's polite. And he's a generous man, I know, very much so. That's never nothing. That always counts. For instance, know who came to see me yesterday?"

Eli shook his head.

"Sean. He's been home a week."

"I know. I drove Marcia down to Boston to collect him. Carl had to work."

"'Course, he's got to take it easy. But he's out of trouble, got a clean bill of health. So, that's something good. Nothing bad about that."

"No."

"Mind you, his hair all fell out. He basically doesn't have any hair. Some fuzz."

"Don't worry," said Eli. "His hair will grow back."

"I'm not worried. Fact is, I approve. Sean's the only boy in the valley would look better with more hair."

They sat for a moment in silence. Then,

"Marcia told me Langdon Taft paid all their bills," said Calpurnia.

"That's right, he did."

"She said you fixed that up with him."

"I talked to him, that's all. I told him what their situation was. He agreed to help. Wasn't much to it, really."

"Was for Sean," said Calpurnia. "Was for Marcia, for Sean's grandma."

"And that's another question I had, right there," said Eli.

"What's that?"

"What happened between her, Marcia's mother, and Langdon?"

"You mean Mollie? Long time ago. She dumped him."

"I got that. Why? What happened?"

"Gave him his walking papers. Left him at the altar."

"Not really?"

"Near enough," said Calpurnia. "Why? Well, what have I been telling you? Can you blame her? One thing, a big thing—Mollie's parents were very strict, stern Sunday people. Lots of church, there. Teetotal? Oh, my, yes. They thought Langdon was pretty wild. Well, he was. They didn't like him at all. Didn't think he was—I don't know—sound. Safe. In spite of his money. This was no President Taft they were getting; it was no Supreme Court judge. And then, I always thought his parents were involved, too, from the other direction, as you might say."

"Langdon's parents?"

"Langdon's. They were something. You remember them."

"Not really," said Eli.

"The old man had a very high opinion of himself. Very high. But why? His own father, your friend's grandad, was nothing but a jumped-up stock clerk for the hardware, but Langdon's father had the brain of Almighty God, according to himself, anyway. And his wife, Langdon's mother? She was from New York, Connecticut, I don't know, but she had her nose so far up in the air she bumped into low tree branches. Nobody could stand them. I guess Mollie finally took a good look and thought, 'Do I really want to deal with that pair for the rest of their lives?' Langdon being an only child, you see. She threw him overboard, and six months later she married Galen Hoover. They all lived happily ever after."

"Except Langdon," said Eli.

"Come on," said Calpurnia. "You saying he's been out there broken-hearted, all these years?"

"Well, he never married."

"No more did I. Am I broken-hearted?"

"It doesn't seem as if."

"I should say it doesn't. But as far as your friend, he's not exactly pining away, is he? It's not like he hadn't had plenty of women in and out of there, one time or another."

"Not that I ever saw," said Eli. "What are you talking about?"

"I've heard what I've heard."

"But you don't know for sure."

"How would I?"

"One way I can think of," said Eli.

"You hush," said Calpurnia. "Just hush yourself. Don't you have to be someplace?"

4
NIGHT COURT

N THE VALLEY, THE DISAPPEARANCE OF WESLEY FILLMORE was the cause of little distress and indeed of considerable rejoicing. Wesley figured as a sort of local hero in reverse. His absence compounded negatively, you might have said, for the good of the community. Scale is everything. Where in a larger setting conspicuous saints and sinners, however rare proportionally, may be numerous in absolute terms, in the valley their numbers, like everything else, were small. Therefore, as Taft, pouring himself a light Sir Walter Scott and shaking out the Brattleboro newspaper, remarked to Eli, the same names kept coming up.

"Court filings," said Taft. "The police report. Car wrecks, DUIs, break-ins, drug deals, domestic disputes, fights, assaults. The same half-dozen people must make seventy-five percent of the trouble. The same names, over and over. It's like Shakespeare, isn't it, old sport?"

"I wouldn't know," said Eli. "Who have we got today?"

Taft returned to the paper. He read. "Well, for example," he said, "here's Katie Harding, twenty-nine. Arrested for fighting with some guy—boyfriend?—doesn't give a name, at the bridge, the swimming place there. She hit him over the head with an ironing board."

"An ironing board?" asked Eli. "What did they have an ironing board for at the swimming hole?"

"Ask Katie. Alcohol was involved, needless to say. As for the ironing board, it might not be the weapon you or I would choose, but Katie made it work. She put the guy in the ER."

"Whatever comes to your hand, I guess," said Eli.

"Then a couple of days later," Taft went on, "here's Katie again, stopped on Route 10 for speeding, DUI, and had a carful of dope. She took a swing at the arresting officer. She and her male companion, both in the lockup."

"Not the same fellow, though, this time, probably," said Eli. "The ironing board fellow?"

"I hope not. But, point is: twice in the same paper? Same girl? I doubt this is her maiden voyage, either."

"I know it isn't," said Eli. "Katie's a frequent flyer. There are others. Look at Wes Fillmore."

"Who?"

"Wesley Fillmore. Don't know Wes? Keep reading the paper, and you will. Jack of all trades, Wes is. Breaking and entering, weed, pills. Mainly, though, Wes is a beater."

"A beater of what?"

"Well, of anything that's within reach, I guess," said Eli. "You know: dogs, cats, horses, other livestock. But specializing in women. Wives, girlfriends, cousins, nieces, sisters. Wes loves to beat up his women. The girls like it, too, it seems. At least, they keep coming back for more. And it's not as if they don't know what they're dealing with. All those boys and girls, Wes, Katie, the others—everybody knows about them. How wouldn't they? It's like you say: those guys are in the paper more than the governor."

"Habitual offenders," said Taft. "It's a demimonde, but it's a little demimonde, a demi-demimonde. When you think about it, that ought to make things easier. Everybody knows who the troublemakers are, everybody knows where they live. Look here, old man: if you could only organize a kind of low-lifes' picnic, and then manage a lightning strike, you could clean the whole plate. You could do a lot of good hereabouts."

"Come on," said Eli. "You're dreaming. You're not going to knock out the whole demitasse in one shot. Won't happen."

"Say it won't. Say you can only knock out one. Even then, you're having an effect. That's what I'm saying: consider the leverage. Look, if you've got a thousand rats in your barn and you shoot one? So what? If you've got three rats in your barn and you shoot one, you've done a good day's work."

"Maybe," said Eli, "but that would be—what do you call it? You can't do it. That's what the courts are for. What about the courts?"

"Have the picnic on a weekend. Courts are closed."

"But still, it's . . . what's the word?"

"The word is vigilantism."

"That's it. It's vigilantism, there. You can't do that. Everybody being his own law? Can't do it."

"But if you *could*, old sport . . ." said Taft.

• • •

Wes didn't like stupid people. He didn't like people who clocked in, did their hours, clocked out, and went home. People who let themselves be taken, hired, used. Dumb fucks who never made a move, never stood up. They made Wes laugh, and they made him mad. The thing about them, Wes said, was that either they didn't know what they wanted, or they didn't want anything. Same difference: dumb fucks, either way.

Wes also didn't like Afros, Jews (he didn't know for sure what one was), Asians, Arabs (he'd never seen one), homos, the rich, the poor, cops—especially cops. Not that Wes was a bigot. As far as Afros, for example, Wes said he didn't have anything against them, he guessed, but they seemed to be a pain in the ass: to want and get a lot from everybody else, to be angry all the time. That was Wes's impression of Afros, anyway. He'd admit he didn't know for sure. The fact is, there were few or none of them to be seen in Wes's world, in the valley, and so Wes couldn't really say.

No, there were no Afros in the valley, Wes knew, and so it was a little odd that tonight he should find himself riding in the rear seat of a police cruiser on his way to he had no idea where, with an enormous uniformed Afro trooper beside him and another driving.

Half an hour earlier, Wes had come off the interstate and headed toward the valley, with a thousand pink ones under his floor mat. Somewhere out in the middle of the woods near Dead River he'd come around a bend to find the cruiser parked across the road with its flashers going. "Oh man?" said Wes. He slowed. Could he turn around and fade back the way he'd come? No chance. The trooper, in Wes's headlights, was motioning for him to pull over. Wes did. The trooper approached. Wes got a look at him, looked again. The trooper was black. Black, and fucking huge: six and a half feet, nearer seven, and two-fifty, two-seventy-five, shaved-headed, a little gold earring in his right ear, the buttons practically popping off the trooper uniform stretched across his massive chest, and a big .45 Colt on his right hip. No question, Wes was impressed.

"Turn off your engine, please, sir," the trooper said. Wes did.

"Exit the vehicle, please, sir," said somebody on Wes's other side. He turned to his right. At the passenger's-side window was another trooper, also black, also enormous: same size, same build, same uniform, same earring, same sidearm. Wes got out of the truck. He waited for the troopers to bring out their breath machine, but,

"This way, sir," said the first trooper.

"Wait a minute," said Wes, but the other trooper took him by his upper arm, pulled him out of his truck, and frog-walked him to the cruiser. He got in the rear with Wes, the first trooper drove, and the three of them set out into the darkness, leaving Wes's truck beside the road.

"Where fuck are we going?" Wes asked.

"Court," said the trooper beside him. "You got a court date."

"Bullshit, court," said Wes. "At three a.m.? No court's on at three a.m."

"This one is," said the trooper.

"This one's night court," said the driver. "Hee-hee."

"Heh-heh," said the trooper in the rear.

Presently, the cruiser turned into a lane and stopped before a large old house with one light on in a room downstairs. Wes knew the house. He'd broken into it once. Got zip. No guns, no cash, no cameras, no TV, nothing but a case of Scotch that Wes tried to sell to Rusty MacLeod for his stupid haggis parties, but Rusty didn't want the stuff, said it was a shit brand. Dry fucking hole, then, for Wes. He thought he'd better act as if the place was strange to him.

"What's this?" he asked.

"Taft's," said the driver. "You know. You been here."

"Not me," said Wes. "I've never seen the place."

The driver turned slowly in his seat. He didn't speak, but he fixed Wes with a long, wide, unblinking gaze.

"I might have driven by," said Wes.

"You been here, and you taken the man's liquor," said the driver. "Must be you forgot? Did you forget?"

"I forgot," said Wes.

"Same way you forgot what you got in your ride under the mat, there, right?" asked the trooper at Wes's side.

"Huh?"

"Same way you forgot what—"

"That's not mine," Wes began, but the driver turned off the cruiser's engine. "It don't matter now," he said. "Let's go."

The trooper at Wes's side opened the door, and the three of them left the car and went to the house, the two gorillas tightly flanking Wes.

They went into a room in the front, a kind of office. There was dim yellow light from a lamp in a corner. Across the room, a desk, with a straight chair in front of it. One of Wes's guards went to the desk and switched on another lamp. He nodded toward the chair, indicating Wes should take it. Wes didn't think so. He'd been pushed around enough tonight. He stood his ground. Then the trooper on his right took him by his right arm, and the other came around and took him by his left, and they lifted him off his feet. Wes hadn't been pushed around enough, after all, it looked like. The troopers moved him to the chair and sat him down, hard.

One of the troopers went to a door in the wall behind and to one side of the desk and knocked. Then he came back to Wes. Wes sat in the visitor's chair facing the desk, with a trooper at each shoulder and slightly behind him.

The door opened. Langdon Taft stepped into the room and went to the desk. He sat. He looked at Wes and his guards. "Alright," he said, and the men took a couple of steps backward, away from Wes in his chair, but not far. Taft looked at Wes. He nodded.

Langdon Taft, a man for whom Wes had no respect. Sure, he knew him. Had been a schoolteacher, wasn't even that any more. A famous drunk. An old fool, a pussy, a little like a rich man, with a rich man's name, a rich man's talk, but having no money (teachers got paid squat), drove an old beater truck, had that whole big house and nothing in it worth stealing, and was therefore, to Wes, no better than another dumb fuck.

Wes had no use for Langdon Taft, and ordinarily he

would have let him know it. He would have stood up where he was, whipped it out, and pissed all over Taft's antique desk. But with those two black linebackers at his rear, he didn't. Plus, he'd admit, Taft had him a little spooked. Taft was supposed to be a drinker. He was supposed to be shit-face drunk twenty-four/seven. He didn't look drunk to Wes, not tonight. He looked stone sober now. He was looking at Wes steadily, wordlessly, across the desk, a look calm, patient, but very level. Very fucking level, cold, as though he, Taft, knew the score here, and so did the others. Only Wes did not. Only Wes didn't know what all this was about.

"What's all this about?" he asked Taft.

Ask him what he thinks it's about, Dangerfield whispered. He had slipped into the room after Taft. Now he stood in the shadows. He was got up in full antique judicial style: white powdered wig, long black robes that swept the floor at his heels as he moved to take his station behind Taft's chair. A high-court judge. *Ask him,* whispered Dangerfield.

"What do you think it's about?" Taft asked Wes.

"Fuck if I know," said Wes. "I didn't ask to be here. All I know, I'm driving home, minding my own business— and here are these two big fuckers. These fucking troopers."

"They aren't troopers," said Taft.

"Well," said Wes, "if they ain't troopers, what are they, then?"

"Meet BZ and Ash," said Taft. "They're officers of the court."

You might call them bailiffs, muttered Dangerfield.

"You might call them bailiffs," Taft told Wes.

"What's that?" Wes asked.

Taft didn't answer him. He opened a drawer in his desk and took out a folder. He took a pair of half-glasses from his pocket, put them on, and made a business of leafing through the papers in the folder. He looked over his glasses at Wes.

"Couple of matters here," he said. "Quite a few, in fact."

"What matters? What the fuck matters?"

Taft referred to the folder again. He turned pages. "Matter of Karin VanBuren Fillmore, for one. Your wife."

"Ex-wife," said Wes. "I haven't seen that skank in years."

"Matter of Brytney Arthur," Taft went on. "Matter of two different restraining orders she filed on you."

"That dumb slut," said Wes. "So, okay, we had a fight. Didn't I tell her? I told her thirty plants, max. Not twenty-nine, not thirty-one. So somebody tips them, and they come out, and they pull up thirty-five plants. She's too dumb to count to thirty. But who goes down? The slut? No. Me. I do. So, yes, we had a little disagreement about that. I already took the hit for that. That's over."

"Cherie Monroe," Taft read on.

"That bitch."

"Broken jaw, multiple contusions. Another restraining order."

"So, I caught her in the rack with my little brother. Kid's thirteen. What was I supposed to do, give her a Teacher of the Year prize?"

"Valerie Cleveland," Taft read.

"Whore," said Wes.

He's repetitious, sighed Dangerfield.

"Krystyn Garfield."

"Bitch."

Very repetitious.

"You're repetitious," said Taft.

"Say what?" Wes asked him.

"You repeat yourself. You already had one bitch."

"Buddy, I've had bitches all over the state."

"He doesn't get it," said Taft. Dangerfield only shook his head.

"You know what?" cried Wes. "Fuck you. Who do you think you fucking are, you know? I know my rights. What is this? Is this a trial?"

"That's right," said Taft.

"Bullshit," said Wes. "I don't see no judge. I don't see no lawyers. I don't see no jury. What kind of a trial is that?"

"The new kind," said Taft.

The old kind, muttered Dangerfield in Taft's ear.

"Hee-hee," said the bailiff to Wes's right.

"Heh-heh," said the bailiff to his left.

"The old kind," said Taft. "It's the kind of trial you don't see much any more. It's a one-man show. Me. I'm the judge. I'm the lawyers. I'm the jury."

Wes tried to rise. He grasped the arms of the chair he sat on and tried to raise himself, but the bailiff on his left put a heavy hand on his left shoulder, and the bailiff on his right put a heavy hand on his right shoulder, and they held Wes down. He struggled briefly, then gave up.

"Okay," he said to Taft. "Okay, okay. I'm cool. You and your big nigger buddies. You got them, you're pretty tough, ain't you? I'd like to see how you'd do without them. I'd like to see that."

Show him, whispered Dangerfield.

Taft nodded to the two standing behind Wes's chair. They withdrew.

Tell him to come ahead.

"Come ahead," said Taft.

Wes glanced over his shoulder. His guards had stepped back. He tensed in his chair.

He's going to jump now, murmured Dangerfield. *When he does, take him down.*

"What do you mean, take him down? Take him down, how?"

With the Talents, said Dangerfield. *Like this.* He made a little flicking motion with his fingers, as though he brushed a stray thread off the sleeve of his robe. *Try it,* he said.

Now Wes started to spring from his chair at Taft. Awkwardly, Taft made the little brush-away motion in imitation of Dangerfield. Wes leapt to his feet—and collapsed on the carpet in front of Taft's desk, simply, abruptly crumpled, as though his legs and knees had turned to tissue paper and folded up beneath him. He hit the floor and sprawled on the carpet.

Oops, said Dangerfield.

Wes tried to get up, and fell back to the floor, his body below the waist quite useless, the legs dragging like the cotton legs of an unstrung marionette. He tried to raise himself on his arms, but his upper body now seemed to have the weight of a stone ledge. He was sweating. He regarded Taft. "Who are you?" he asked.

Tell him.

"You tell him," said Taft.

"What?" asked Wes.

He can't hear me.

"You're crazy, you know that?" Wes told Taft. "You are a fucking nutjob. Talking to yourself. Talking to nobody. You think I'm scared of you? Of a dumb fuck, of a retard? You think I'm scared of your apes? Fuck them. Fuck them, and fuck you."

"That's the stuff," said Taft. "Show a little spirit. Show us you'd rather die on your feet than live on your knees."

"Fucking-A right, I would," said Wes.

"Show us you'd rather reign in hell than serve in heaven," said Taft.

"Huh?"

"Show us what a ball of fire you are," said Taft, "a rebel angel."

Him? muttered Dangerfield. *This twerp? No chance.*

"A regular woodchuck Lucifer," Taft went on.

Not even close, hissed Dangerfield.

Taft nodded, and the two bailiffs took Wes by the arms and picked him up off the floor. They returned him to his seat. Wes slumped in the chair. He felt his legs. They had been paper; now they were wood. They felt like sticks tied to his trunk with string. Whatever force he'd had a minute ago was gone. He looked at Taft.

"All those women," said Taft. "Those poor dumb women. All that trouble. Your trouble. What about that?"

Wes was panting like a dog. He was panting out of fear.

"Okay," he said. "Okay. I know I got a terrible temper. I go apeshit. More than I should. So, that's just me, you know? I don't mean nothing. I know I've hurt people. I'm sorry for that. Okay?"

"What does counsel have to say?" asked Taft.

The bailiff on Wes's left spoke up. Was he the one Taft had called BZ, or was he the other, the one called Ash? "Your honor," he said, "this brother never had a chance. Way he was raised up himself? Daddy beat on mama, grandpa beat on granny. You see that at home, you do the same. That's all it is."

"You're saying he's not responsible?" Taft asked the bailiff.

"Did I say that, your honor? Damn straight, he's responsible. He did what he did, didn't he?"

Taft turned to the bailiff on Wes's right.

"Youngblood just told you he's sorry," the bailiff said. "He's repentant. He's remorseful. Ain't you?" He put his broad, heavy hand on Wes's shoulder and pressed him down further in his chair.

"I am," cried Wes. "I swear to God, I am. I swear to Christ!"

That'll do, snapped Dangerfield.

"He won't never do it again, your honor," said the bailiff. "Nothing like he did. It won't happen again, none of it, ever."

He's got that right, at least.

"He's got that right," said Taft.

"Wait!" said Wes. "Oh, God, wait a minute!"

The bailiff on his left tried one last time. "Your honor," he said to Taft. "Can you ignore this brother's remorse? Don't it matter to you that he repents, that he's contrite, that he promises to reform? Can't there be no mercy in this court?"

Not that kind of court, is it? purred Dangerfield. *You want mercy, well, you might try the competition, I suppose. We don't stock it.* Taft merely shook his head and busied himself with his folder of papers relating to Wesley Fillmore. Briskly, all business now, he squared the papers up and let the folder drop on his desk with a slap.

"Alright," said Taft. The bailiffs took Wes and raised him out of his chair. They looked at Taft. Taft nodded, and the two turned Wes toward the door of the study, toward the shadows in the recesses of the room. Wes's toes dragged behind him over the carpet.

"Wait," squeaked Wes.

Lose this creep, said Dangerfield.

Again, as though he brushed a fly off the surface of his desk, Taft flicked his hand toward the door. The bailiffs, with Wes captive between them, led him to the door and out of the room. The door shut behind them.

Taft and Dangerfield sat silently. After a moment, "Where will they take him?" Taft asked.

You know where, Chief.

"I guess I do," said Taft.

You feel badly for him?

"Maybe."

You want him back?

"No. I don't. Though, come to that, I suppose I might be seeing him one of these days, where he's going."

Not likely, said Dangerfield.

"Oh? Why not?"

Big place, where he's going.

"Long trip?"

He's already there, Chief.

• • •

"Just gone," said Eli.

"Is that right, old boy?" Taft asked.

"His place?" said Eli. "Door's not even locked. His stuff's all there, clothes, food in the fridge, his stash. His truck's parked out in the boonies—not far from you, matter of fact. Unlocked, pretty good payload of painkillers hidden in the cab. No Wes. Nobody's seen him for, what, a week?"

"Well," said Taft, "from what you said, he won't be missed. Can I pour you one?"

"Just a short one," said Eli. "No, he won't," he went on. "Sheriff's tickled. Best he can think, Wes and some of his friends had a disagreement, and it didn't end well for Wes. But you wouldn't expect that to mean Wes would be gone for good. He and his friends don't usually take things that far."

"So you think he'll be back someday?"

"It's possible," said Eli. "Sheriff's cautiously optimistic. But it's almost too good to be true, isn't it? Fellows like Wes? They're always there, aren't they? You never really get rid of them."

"Mmm."

"Funny, isn't it?" Eli went on, "how we were talking about Wes just the other day?"

"Mmm."

"We were saying how if Wes were to go away, just go away, that wouldn't be a bad thing," said Eli.

"Were we, old sport?"

5

BEASTS ON THE BUS

UP IN THE FRONT, WHERE HE SAT WITH THE OTHER LITTLE ones, Toby turned in his seat and looked at the big girl. Suddenly she and her sister and their cousin had shut up and left poor Lucas alone. Toby looked again. The new driver was there. He was with the girls. He was doing something. What was the new driver doing? *What?*

The bus had pulled into a turnout and stopped. The driver, whom Toby had never seen before, had gone back toward the rear and was talking in a low voice to some of the older kids. Toby looked at the big girl, Mandy. He was afraid of Mandy. They all were.

Toby was seven and a half. He didn't miss much, and here was something new. *What?* The school bus, normally a loud, clamoring barnyard of voices and misbehavior, had gone quite silent, quite still. The other younger kids at the front turned in their seats and looked. Toby was afraid to look. He couldn't look. He looked. Sitting in Mandy's seat, wearing Mandy's leather jacket and Mandy's backpack, and having even some sense about its expression of Mandy's hardened gaze, was, unmistakably, a dusky, wrinkled, warted, and hideous amphibian—and not an ordinary amphibian, but about a two-hundred-pounder—Mandy, herself, being a heavy girl. *What?*

For the first month of school, Toby and the other grade schoolers had watched the Grant twins, Mandy and Candy, and their cousin, TJ Bush, tag-team poor Lucas Polk. They had watched as Mandy, Candy, and TJ worked Lucas the way a small family of timber wolves might work a motherless moose calf surrounded on a frozen pond. Morning and afternoon, as Lucas boarded the bus and made his way to the rear, Mandy tripped him. As he stumbled farther back, Candy hip-checked him into the kids in the seats to his right, causing them to shove him back into the aisle. When Lucas at last made it to his seat, TJ, immediately behind him, reached forward and snatched his hat, or, if Lucas wasn't wearing a hat (guess why he seldom did), TJ grabbed his hair, yanking, and slapped his head back and forth from behind—playful slaps, arguably, but hard.

"Careful," Mandy called to TJ. "Don't get him mad. Don't get Lucas mad. He might tell his dad on you."

"I ain't scared of his dad," said TJ.

"You should be," said Candy. "Hey, Lucas, shouldn't he be scared of your dad?"

"But his dad ain't around," said TJ.

"That's right," said Candy. "Lucas's dad ain't around. Where is he, Lucas?"

"He's in the joint," said TJ.

"The what? What's that you say, cousin?"

"The slam. Lucas's dad's in the slam. He's in the big house. Ain't he, Lucas?"

"Warden! Warden!" cried Candy.

"Is that right, Lucas?" said Mandy. "Hey, Lucas? Hey? I'm talking to you. Where is your dad, anyway?"

"Fuck you," said Lucas.

"Ooh! Lucas said fuck! Lucas said fuck!"

"Warden! Lucas said fuck!"

"Where is he, Lucas? Where is your dad at?"

"Warden! Warden!"

Fifteen, twenty minutes: the ride between home and school took that long, no more. You can stand anything for fifteen, twenty minutes. Can't you? Lucas looked out the window or he looked at the floor. The ride to school was better than the ride home. No, it wasn't. Fifteen, twenty minutes: Lucas's daily, rolling hell. And if it didn't stack up very high beside other, older, more celebrated, more adult hells, still, it was no fun for Lucas.

• • •

"Poor kid," said Taft. "How is it you know him?"

"His mom's my cousin Sally," said Eli. "She's had a tough time, every way. Now it's her boy. They won't leave him be."

"Bullies," said Taft. "I saw it at school. They're like sharks. They can smell a quarter-teaspoon of blood in the Gulf of Mexico. They go right after it. They tear away at it until there's nothing left."

"Somebody ought to stop them," said Eli.

"But how, exactly? That's the thing, old boy. There's

nothing to stop. It's a word, a tone of voice, a look, a little shove in the hall, a moment. You can forbid it, but that's not stopping it. The kids doing it, the bullies, have to stop it. They have to change."

"Well, then somebody ought to change them, then," said Eli.

"Somebody ought to, old sport," said Taft.

• • •

Poor Lucas. Taft was right. The school couldn't protect him from Mandy and Candy and TJ. The teachers couldn't. The bus driver couldn't. You would think he might. You would think a rural school bus in transit ought to be like a vessel on the high seas: a universe apart, self-contained, charged with a precious cargo, and therefore necessarily subject to a captain whose authority is absolute. Not at all. Old Bob Buchanan, the regular driver, was a vague, mild soul who had learned that the kids of today would eat him alive unless he remained invisible. They would eat him alive; or if they didn't, their parents would. Bob knew what went on among his riders. He knew Mandy and Candy and TJ. He knew them too well. He wished he could help Lucas Polk. He knew he could not.

Time was, he might have. Time was, if a kid was out of line, Bob would have pulled over and kicked him the hell off the bus; let him walk home. No more. Kids didn't get out of line today. Schools did, principals and teachers did, bus drivers did. Not kids. Today if you kicked an out-of-line kid off your bus, you'd soon have an angry mom on your doorstep. If she didn't hear what she wanted to hear, she'd be back tomorrow with her lawyer. Bob was looking at five years to retirement, with luck, four. Therefore he drove the bus: he opened the door, he closed the door. Bob knew what went on behind him. But he reckoned the hell that began at his back was Lucas's hell, it wasn't Bob's.

Where was he, Bob, anyway? Young Toby had watched as Langdon Taft (for the strange driver that day was he) cut the engine of the bus, set the brake, left the driver's seat, and walked down the aisle to where Lucas sat studying the floor between his feet. Taft stopped.

Lucas looked up. He saw a tall, thin-built man, older, not from school. Nobody he knew.

"You get this every day?" Taft asked him.

"Get what?" asked Lucas.

"This," said Taft. "Does this happen every day? With them?" He glanced at Candy and Mandy in their seat a couple of rows toward the rear. They were quiet.

"Pretty much," said Lucas.

"Why do you take it?"

Lucas shrugged.

"Why don't you do something?"

"I did," said Lucas. "Once I punched TJ. That made it worse."

Taft nodded. "I suppose it did," he said. "Let me try?"

"No," said Lucas. "That would make it worse worse. A teacher? A grownup? They'll just wait till you're not here. Then it will be worse."

"Not this time. This time's different."

"How?"

"Watch," said Taft.

He turned to Mandy and Candy. The bus was silent. TJ, in the seat behind Lucas, watched. Taft stood over the twins.

"Get off," he said.

"What?" said Mandy.

"Get off. Your ride's over."

"What do you mean, get off?"

Taft was silent.

"Who are you?" Candy asked him.

"Friend of Lucas's," said Taft.

"Lucas?" said Mandy. "What's he been telling you? We don't mean nothing. We're just fucking with him. Lucas knows that. Right, Lucas?"

"Get off," said Taft again.

"You mean, here?" Mandy asked. "You mean, now?" Her voice broke a little. "How are we supposed to get home?"

Dangerfield sat on the long seat in the very back of the bus. He wore the rusty scholar's gown of an old-fashioned schoolmaster, with a scholar's tasseled mortarboard cocked on his head and a long wooden rod in his hand for a pointer. He pointed the rod at Mandy. *Tell her to hop*, he whispered.

"Hop," said Taft.

Not that way, sighed Dangerfield. *The Talents, the Talents. Bring the Talents.*

As Dangerfield had instructed him to do with Wesley Fillmore, Taft made an odd, fastidious little gesture in Mandy and Candy's direction, as though he dusted a bit of lint off his sleeve toward them. Watching, little Toby saw that both the Grants, even as they sat in their places, had been changed. He hadn't seen them change, but he saw that they had changed. They had been transformed. They had been turned from loud, strapping, jeering high school girls into large and loathsome batrachians.

"Go," said Taft.

Mandy and Candy slid out of their seat and fell to the floor with a double plop, then, too stout to hop easily, they commenced to belly-flop their way to the front. Together they tumbled down the steps and out of the bus onto the gravel of the turnout, and began feebly hopping away down the road, Mandy ahead, Candy following.

In the bus, Taft wasn't finished. He turned to TJ Bush. "Are you going with them?" he asked.

"No, sir," said TJ.

"Do you want to go with them?"

"No, sir."

"You don't have much to say, do you?"

"No, sir."

He did a minute ago, muttered Dangerfield.

"You did," said Taft. "When you were going after my friend Lucas. You had a lot to say then. 'Where's your father, Lucas?' you asked. 'He's in the joint,' you said. 'He's in the big house,' you said. Did you think that was funny?"

"No, sir," said TJ.

"Why say it, then?"

"I don't know."

Dangerfield pointed his rod at TJ. *Watch him lay it off on the girls*, whispered Dangerfield.

"I know," said Taft to TJ. "Those girls."

"Yes, sir," said TJ. "That's it, sir. It was them. They always want to shit on Lucas, not me. We won't do it any more, though."

Dangerfield stood, leaned forward, and cracked TJ over the head with his pointer. "Ow," cried TJ, ducking.

"That's true," said Taft, "you won't do it any more." He glanced at Dangerfield and nodded once, then turned and went back forward. He stopped at Lucas's seat again. "What do you think?" he asked the boy.

Lucas regarded him. "I don't know," he said.

"They're gone," said Taft.

"TJ isn't gone."

"TJ's finished. They all are."

"Maybe."

Taft smiled. "You're a skeptic," he said.

"Maybe."

"You'll see," said Taft. Lucas didn't reply.

Taft returned to the driver's seat. He started the engine, let off the brake, and got back on the road. As the bus passed Mandy and Candy, flopping and lurching along the roadside, somebody in the rear began to clap. Soon the entire bus was cheering.

Little Toby was seated near the driver. "Hey," he said.

Taft drove the bus.

"Hey," said Toby again.

"You aren't supposed to talk to the driver," said Taft. "It's distracting."

"You aren't the driver, though. Bob is."

"True," said Taft.

"Where is Bob?"

"Day off."

"Were they toads or frogs?" asked Toby. "Mandy and Candy."

"Toads."

"They looked more like frogs."

"Toads."

"Will they always be toads from now on? Mandy and Candy? Are they toads for good?"

"I doubt it," said Taft. "The toads wouldn't have them."

"So they'll be back to how they were before?"

"No," said Taft.

• • •

Taft was right. Mandy and Candy were in school the next day, and they were in human form (or what, with them, passed for human form); but they were much subdued, and subdued they remained. When not in class, they practically lived in the office of the school psychiatrist. In the halls of the school, if they met Lucas, they shrank to the wall and sidled fearfully past. On the bus they were mute and harmless. TJ was the same. Then it was learned that the girls' father had taken a job upstate. He moved the family, and Mandy and Candy were to be seen in the valley no more. TJ was sent to a military school, where he was reported to be doing very well.

It was young Toby, in later years, to whom the incident on the bus when the Grant twins were silenced returned; Toby who experienced it again and again in his memory, puzzled over it, and tried to account for it. What had happened that day? What had he seen? Was Mandy and Candy's transformation some kind of conjuror's trick, an irresistible illusion? Who was the illusionist? Taft? Hard to believe. Someone else, then? Who? Nobody else was there. Nobody? Who was it in the back seat, then, whom Taft had nodded to at the end? That seat had been empty. Was somebody there?

At seven and a half, Toby didn't miss much. He knew what he had seen. It was no magic trick. The girls, the toads, were real. But he got no further. How could he? He had no hold. Taft gave him none. That afternoon on the bus, as Taft drove along to complete the route, minus Mandy and Candy, Toby hadn't left off questioning him. He got nowhere.

"What happened?" Toby asked him.

Careful, whispered Dangerfield. He stood by the doors of the bus, to Taft's right.

"What do you mean?" Taft asked Toby.

"Mandy and Candy. What happened?"

"Nothing."

"Yes, it did, too. You did it. How did you do it?"

"Do what?" asked Taft.

"You know what. Turn them into frogs."

"Toads."

"Turn them into toads. How did you do that?"

"I told you before," said Taft, "don't distract the driver."

Good, chuckled Dangerfield, *that's good, Chief*—and he struck the dashboard of the bus a happy smack with his wooden pointer.

6

SORRY FOR CATS

PASTOR CHET CARTER, OF THE VALLEY GOSPEL CHAPEL, told his flock that, without the Lord, the condition of a man or a woman in this, our life, is utter solitude. We are born alone, we die alone—absent the Lord. He is present at our comings hither, and he is present at our goings hence: He and only He. Thus the doctrine of Pastor Chet.

Calpurnia Lincoln said Pastor Chet was full of it. "Born alone?" she said. "Nonsense."

"You think?" Eli asked her. He had come by the Hospice for a visit with Calpurnia. She sat in the easy chair by the window of her little room. Eli perched on the windowsill.

"Bald-headed nonsense," said Calpurnia. "I know. I was born at home. We all were, at the old place on Bible Hill. I helped my mother when my brothers and sisters were born; at least I was there. Were any of us born alone? Nonsense. Mother was there, after all."

"That isn't what Pastor Chet's talking about, though, is it?" asked Eli. "I don't think your mother counts."

"She might have thought she did, in the circumstances," said Calpurnia. "Being she was the one having the baby. But, come on. Alone? It was like a party. There were a couple of aunts, cousins, the midwife, mother's canary bird—you know: first came the doctor, then came the nurse, then came the lady with the alligator purse. Quite a crowd. Born alone? I should say not."

"All that help. Where was your father?"

"Out in the barn buying drinks for the cows, probably. That's where he was whenever he could be."

"I liked your father," said Eli.

"My father died in 1940," said Calpurnia. "You weren't even born. But as for dying, dying alone, same thing. Nonsense. Look at this place. You can't turn around without somebody coming along to bring you your meds, your lunch; coming to change your linen, wash your windows, clip your toenails, do your hair; somebody wants to play some Hearts, watch the ballgame, visit. Dying? Well, sure, I guess. That's what this place is, isn't it? That's why we're here. Dying alone? No. Far from it. Mind you, I'm not criticizing. It's alright here. I like it fine. But alone? Phooey."

"You're right about that," said Eli. "You've got everything in here. Even animals. I saw a dog downstairs."

"That's Ringo. Belongs to one of the girls. Cindy? I think he's Cindy's. She brings him in to see people, get us all cheered up. Works, too. It's a new thing they do."

"A dog in a clinic? A dog in a hospital? Is that sanitary? I don't know if I approve of that."

"I don't know if anybody cares whether you approve of it or not," said Calpurnia. "We're glad to have him,

Ringo. I'm glad. That's one thing I miss about this place, is my dogs. Do you remember any of my dogs?"

"I remember your cat. I remember Snowflake."

"Snowflake was a rabbit. He was Ruthie's rabbit. That was later. The cat was Snowball, but she wasn't mine. She lived in the barn."

"Before my time."

"Long before," said Calpurnia. "No, I never wanted a cat. Cats made me feel bad. They still do. I feel sorry for cats. There was a thing, once, at home, I can't have been more than seven, eight. The cat had kittens. That could have been Snowball, come to think, or a Snowball. We had a whole line of Snowballs. Barn cats. So, we had Mrs. Pierce, from over the hill, helping in the kitchen for some reason that day, and she brought the new kittens in a basket and put them on the porch, outside, asked me did I want to play with them. Well, sure. There were five or six of them, some white, some black. They couldn't have been more than a couple of days old. They had these round blue eyes, like kittens do, with that surprised, shocked look that kittens have, like granny just broke wind, and they tussled around and rolled themselves into a ball, and crawled into my lap and all up and down of me. We had a fine old time out on the porch. But then the kittens got tired, and I guess so did I, and Mrs. Pierce asked me was I about done playing with them, and I said I was—thinking, you know, that they were mine now and I could play with them whenever I liked. But Mrs. Pierce said, 'Alright, then, if you're finished with them.' And she put the kittens in a feed sack and took and drowned them in the cold spring. Just like that. Tossed the sack over the bank. Those kittens hadn't any use any more, you see. So she got rid of them. How did she do that? Easy. She killed them. No, a farm's a cruel place for animals, ask me. You might not think it would be, but it is."

"For kittens, anyway," said Eli. "That farm, anyway."

"For anything," said Calpurnia. "Any farm. The animals are there to be used. The way Father used to say: they're tools. You use them up, you get rid of them. That's unless you eat them. Either way, you kill them."

"Well, but some you don't kill, right? You raise them, you care for them, then you sell them. That's not using them up and getting rid of them."

"Sure, it is. Somebody else kills them, that's all. Comes to the same thing, ask me."

"You're a bright ray of sunshine today, ain't you?"

"Sure, I am," said Calpurnia. "Like always. No: I am. I'm fine. I'm not down today, not any day. But it doesn't do to be too sentimental about life, is what I'm saying. There are hard things. It doesn't do to pour syrup over them and make believe they're griddle cakes. That's all."

"Pastor Chet, tell you the same thing, I bet," said Eli.

"Don't give me Pastor Chet."

"I'll be sure and tell him what a high opinion you have of him."

"He knows," said Calpurnia. "And don't be telling me you spend a lot of time in church, either, his or anybody else's. I know different."

"Oh, you do? How?"

"Polly. Polly Jefferson. She goes to Pastor Chet's chapel. She says she's never seen you there, not once."

"So what if she hasn't? Maybe I go to some other church."

"No, you do not," said Calpurnia. "Polly would have seen you."

"What if I was going to a church she doesn't go to?"

"There aren't any," said Calpurnia. "She goes to all of them. Takes more than one church to hold Polly."

One of the Hospice housekeeping staff stood in the doorway to the sun porch. "You're all set," she told Calpurnia.

"Thank you, dear," said Calpurnia. To Eli she said, "I know how busy you are. You probably want to get on your way."

"No," said Eli. "I've got nothing till late afternoon."

"Well, then, get something," said Calpurnia. Eli stood.

"Just switch on the TV on your way out, would you?" asked Calpurnia.

"What's on?"

"*Jeopardy.*"

"That's that quiz show," said Eli. "I had to give up on that one. Lots of the questions, I know the answers, alright, but I have to think for a second. Then somebody else answers. They go too quick for me."

"Me, too," said Calpurnia. "I like the boss, though. He's a gentleman. Plus, I think he's good looking."

"He don't do it for me," said Eli, and he left Calpurnia with the familiar lilting music coming up in the little room.

7

ELI'S WAY

ASKED FOR IT, THOUGHT TAFT. WALKED RIGHT INTO IT. Give the devil a task, he will perform it. Give the devil a test, he will pass. Devil? What devil? Not much of a devil. A sleight-of-hand man, a tawdry conjuror. Half the taxi drivers in Vegas could no doubt do as well. Still, what about that suddenly healthy kid, that happy billing office at Mass General, that little jerk deleted—simply deleted? What about those bailiffs? Those toads? Place an order, and the devil will fulfill. Send out the invitations, and the devil will attend. Asked for it, alright. Asked for it, and got it.

Disappointing, though. Not what might have been predicted. You expect a certain level of dramaturgy, don't you? A certain gravity? And, then—nothing. No smoke. No brimstone. No Latin. In the event, crass salesmanship, a squalid businessman. Turns up here like a damned vacuum cleaner agent or, at best, the fellow beside you on a flight, some species of small executive, glib, familiar, able in some small way. Not original. Not serious. And what's this "Chief?" Chief, this, Chief, that. "You've already signed, Chief." "I like your spirit, Chief." Chief? No, by no means serious.

A peasant. ("Common," Mother would say.) Told him so. Can't imagine passing up the bucks, the fun. Not educated. Well, then, he will be. Let him watch. Let him learn. Let him see how a gentleman sells his soul.

The deal? The closing? The final curtain? The carrying down, down, down? The hot place? Not worried. Why? Simple: not a believer. Heaven, hell, reward, punishment, the soul itself (didn't Descartes say even your friends and neighbors, even their dogs and cats, as far as anybody knows for sure?). Fiction. Dreams, fairy tales, fables, unworthy of an intelligent adult. You beat the devil, not by superior play, but by ignoring the game. You don't sell your soul, you mortgage it, but on easy terms. The easiest terms, no terms at all: you borrow gold and pay back air. Less than air. Less than nothing.

One thing, though: Eli. Ought to tell Eli. Feel badly about Eli. Disloyal. Secretive. If Eli were in a fix, he'd tell me, wouldn't he? Would he? Probably not. But, still, point is: an occasion of sympathy, of comfort, of friendship. A gift. A gift of the self. Incompatible with secrecy.

Secrecy, that's the destructive thing. Telling Eli? Dangerfield won't have it, of course. Voids the bargain, didn't he say? Secretive? He lives in secret. He *is* a secret. He's more: he is a secret in himself, and he is the cause that secrecy is in other men. He wouldn't stand for my telling. Well?

Break the secret, then. Tell Eli. A good man, Eli. Feet on the ground, but no simpleton. Versatile. Turn his hand to anything: work on the roads, heavy equipment, concrete, building, masonry, stonework, even wiring. Eli can take it on. He can scope the business out, hitch his trousers, and put up a decent job—not elegant, but sound and serviceable. I? The other way: could only ever do one thing, and never had any clear idea what that thing was. Rather be like Eli, but like Eli, Eli's way, you can't sell your soul to be.

Must tell Eli, but how? "See here, Eli, old sport, sit down—no, there. Good. Drink? Didn't think so. Um, ah, well, it's like this, Eli: I've made a pact with Satan. I am damned, Eli, lost, fallen, anathema, cast into the outer darkness." Like that? Wouldn't believe me. Don't believe myself.

Ah, here he comes.

Outside the window, in the yard, Eli was taking a chainsaw from his truck. He'd put it on the tailgate and was gassing it. He'd come as he said he would to trim the high tree branch that was hitting the house. In a minute, he was in Taft's doorway.

"Get that branch," Eli said.

"Come in, old sport. Have a drink first."

Eli stayed where he was. "Great idea," he said. "Have a couple of drinks, then climb up on a ladder and get started with your chainsaw, see how long you last. Is that an event in the woodchuck rodeo? It should be."

"Something soft? Glass of water?"

"Maybe after," said Eli. But he stayed in the door. "I've been out at Orson's," he said. "I was helping him with his wood. That's how come I have the saw."

"How's Orson?" Taft asked.

"Not too good. He's got the bank after him. He's in default, they say."

"It can't be. It's not possible."

"Sure. That's what I told him. But it's complicated. Orson's note got bought by another bank, and that bank has this fund company—or maybe it's the company has the bank—that says Orson's in default."

"It doesn't matter which bank owns what, old man. Orson's paid up. He can prove it. It's some computer thing."

"They've put him into foreclosure."

"You're joking."

"I'm not, and neither is Orson. The bank told him they're sending their lawyer up from New York to handle their end. They have a court date. Orson better be there, they say."

Taft was silent for a moment, sitting at his desk. Eli stood in the doorway. Presently Taft looked up at him.

"When's he supposed to be in court?" he asked.

"I don't know. Next week sometime."

"What's the name of the bank?"

"Orson didn't say. A New York bank."

"I'll call him. Don't worry. Nothing will happen. No foreclosure. Orson's okay."

"It don't look to me like he's okay," said Eli.

"I tell you that he is. Orson will be fine."

"How do you know that?"

Taft took in a breath. He let it out. He looked at Eli. "Come on in," he said.

Eli came into the room. Taft pointed at the visitor's chair in front of his desk.

"You ask how I know Orson needn't worry," said Taft.

Eli nodded.

"Sit down a minute, old sport," said Taft. "Give me a moment. I'll tell you how I know. It takes some telling. Oh, shut the door, would you?"

"Why?" asked Eli. "Nobody's here, are they?"

"Shut it, anyway, old sport," said Taft.

• • •

Dangerfield rattled the ice in his glass. Taft passed the Sir Walter's.

A New York lawyer? said Dangerfield. *Shouldn't be a problem, Chief. Of course, you never really enjoy taking them on. It's like betting against the home team. Can't be helped. I'll bring the guys. They need work. They're bored.*

"I'll be glad to see them," said Taft.

They'll be glad to see you, too. They think highly of you. They've been missing you, lately. Which brings up a question in my mind.

"A question about what?"

Our contract, Chief. We're working it through, you know.

"I know."

We're moving right along, in fact. Columbus Day? We're half done, better than. You understand that?

"I understand."

You understand, but you seem very cool, very untroubled. That surprises me a little. How is that, Chief?

"Maybe I don't think I have so much to be troubled about."

Dangerfield clapped his hands. *Hah*, he said. *I knew*

it. I knew it. I read you like a book, Chiefy-boy. You think you're immune, don't you? You think hell's a fable. You think it's all trifles and old wives' tales. I've heard it before, Chief. You think you can doubt your way out of our deal. You think you can brain your way out. You think you're too smart for hell. You'll go on thinking it until you find out differently. Don't believe me? Look at me. What am I? What have you seen me do? Have I held up my end, here?

"Yes," said Taft.

A hundred percent?

"Yes."

Whatever you asked for? The sick kid, the wife beater, the bullies. Have I not made good on each and every one of them?

"You've made good."

Could you have worked any of those things on your own?

"No."

No, Chief, you couldn't. For that you need the Talents. We talked about them. The Talents that I have, as you know, that you have from me, and from me alone. You've used them. You've seen what they can do. Where do you think I got them? You think hell's a fable? What are the Talents? What am I? Where did I come from?

"I don't know," said Taft.

I think you do, Chief. If you don't, you'll find out soon enough.

Dangerfield drained his glass. He set it down on Taft's desk with a rap. *Hell's no fable, Chief,* he said. *But from one point of view, it's no big deal, either. My superior would-*

n't like my saying this, but you know me, Chief: I'm for open dealing, and facts are facts. Hell? It's simple, really. Hell's like a DUI. It's like getting behind the wheel when you've had a few. You've done that, I bet.

"Maybe once or twice."

Sure, you have. Everybody does it. You know you shouldn't, but you do it anyway. You know you can get busted, you know that will mean all kinds of no-fun. Doesn't matter: you keep risking it. Why? Because you don't really believe you'll ever get nailed. You don't believe it, and don't believe it—right up to the night when you're standing in the road in the blue flashers, blowing down that little tube they give you, wondering which of your royally pissed off loved ones to tell the cop to call, and thinking, 'Fuck me, what a moron.'

Taft nodded.

Do you get what I'm telling you, here, Chief?

"I get it."

I'm, telling you it will happen, said Dangerfield.

"I know."

Difference is, with the DUI, you don't know when. In your case, you do. You know, because it's in the contract. Columbus Day. Right?

"It's in the contract," said Taft.

8

SHOW BUSINESS

YOUNG LUCAS POLK, THEN THIRTEEN, BROKE INTO McKinley's by knocking down the back door with a sledgehammer. Inside, he used the hammer on one of the coolers and on the deli case. He stole two six-packs of beer, drank one of them there and then, and brought the other out the front. He stole McKinley's truck, backed it through McKinley's plate glass window, drove on, side-swiped McKinley's wife's Cherokee, made the road at last, and then crashed the truck in a pond five miles out.

The people in the house across the road heard the crash and called the authorities. Fortunately for Lucas, Trooper Amy Madison of the state police chanced to be patrolling in the vicinity. She reached the pond as McKinley's truck, with Lucas unconscious in the driver's seat, began to sink. At the water's edge, Trooper Madison didn't hesitate. She jumped into the pond and half-waded–half-swam to the truck. She found the driver's-side window closed, the door jammed immovably shut. Inside the cab, the water had risen to Lucas's chest.

Trooper Madison drew her service revolver and, holding it by the barrel, she used the butt to smash the window. She reached in to Lucas, cut his seatbelt, and lifted him as much farther out of the water as she could. Then, seizing the half-submerged truck with both hands and bracing her feet against the hood and roof, she threw all her weight and all her strength into pulling open the door. The door bent, then gave. The trooper wrenched it open. She took Lucas's limp body by the collar, and heaved him out of the truck. She carried him to the bank. By the time the ambulance arrived, Lucas was awake and shivering in a blanket in the rear of Trooper Madison's cruiser. The trooper herself was beside the road doing deep knee bends to keep her legs loose after their exertion.

Lucas was arrested, his mother was called. The next day it was decided that, owing to his age and lack of any record of misconduct, Lucas wouldn't be prosecuted, but would instead be supervised by the court as he made restitution for the damage he had caused. He would not, however, be making restitution to Storekeeper McKinley. McKinley had consented to the plan for Lucas, but he made it clear he wanted nothing further to do with the boy and in fact swore to have the law on him if he ever again set foot on McKinley's premises. Some other way would have to be found for Lucas to make good.

Eli Adams was Lucas's mother's cousin. He talked to her, then he talked to the magistrate. Then he went to see Langdon Taft. Taft had helped Lucas before; and Eli knew Taft had a big house that hadn't had a fresh coat of paint in at least twenty years. Also, he knew Taft had at one time been a teacher, a fact that suggested to Eli his friend had a level of tolerance for the young. Finally, Eli had recently come to a new appreciation, a new understanding, of certain abilities he found Taft to possess, certain gifts: a gift for persuasion, a gift for resolving difficulties, for helping justice prevail, sometimes roughly, in the obscure affairs of their small community. On behalf of Lucas and his mother, then, Eli went to see Taft.

Alone in the valley, Taft had heard nothing of Lucas's exploit at McKinley's. Eli described it, without stressing the drunkenness, theft, and vandalism involved, and told Taft a little about the boy's situation. An incarcerated father, a desperate, struggling mother, a self-destructive pattern ominously emerging, no friends, no protectors, no oversight—not a bad kid, not at all, a sweet kid, really, and quite bright, but a kid who had taken a long step down a short road. Another time, the authorities (never mind McKinley or his successor) would not go so easy. There needed not to be another time, therefore.

"What's he doing now?" Taft asked Eli.

"He's been put into Diversion."

"Diversion, old sport?"

"Diversion's when they figure out something for you to do so you don't go to jail where you belong."

"Really?" said Taft, "I wish somebody would put me into Diversion. Diversion sounds pretty good."

"It's for youthful offenders, though, mostly," said Eli.

"Pity. Can I give you a small Sir Walter's?"

"I'm good," said Eli.

Eli's idea was that Taft should pay McKinley for the

damages caused by Lucas, and then hire Lucas to paint his house, Taft to supply paint, brushes, ladders, and so on, and to work alongside Lucas, keeping an eye on the boy, gaining his trust, building his confidence. Then, when the job was done, Lucas's wage would go to square his account with Taft, and hence with McKinley, and clear him with the court.

"How much in damages for McKinley are we talking about?" Taft asked Eli.

"Seven-eight grand."

"You love to spend my money, don't you, old sport?"

"Your money?" said Eli. "It ain't your money, is it? Not by what you told me the other day. Go see your new buddy. Go see the Mystery Guest."

"I thought you didn't believe it, about him. You said you didn't."

"I don't know if I do or I don't," said Eli.

"But you're telling me to use him."

"It worked for Sean."

"So it did," said Taft. "Though Sean's case was different, wasn't it? Sean was going to die. This kid? This Luke? This doesn't sound to me like a promising kid. For one thing, he doesn't stay fixed. All the trouble he was having on the school bus? We rode to his rescue. We dealt with the situation. We made a happy ending for him."

"You did," said Eli. "You and your partner."

"We did," said Taft. "And now he's back, worse than before. I don't know: how about this? How about, good luck to this kid, and when I want my house painted, I'll hire a painter, not a juvenile delinquent."

"Luke ain't a juvenile delinquent," said Eli. "He's a

good kid. Promising? Teachers say he's one of the smartest kids they've seen. Luke's alright. He screwed up, is all. You never screwed up?"

"Never, old man."

"He's hit a rough patch," Eli went on. "He needs a break. He needs more than the money for McKinley. He needs a friend. What it is: the kid's depressed."

"Depressed?" said Taft. "Of course he's depressed. Everybody's depressed. I'm depressed. You're depressed."

"I ain't either depressed," said Eli.

"Well, then, maybe you should be. How long is this business going to go on?"

"I don't know," said Eli. "This big old place? All the upkeep you haven't given it over the years? It will have to be scraped down good before you can even think about painting. Say, a week for the scraping. The whole job? Another week, two—that's if the weather holds for you."

"Christ," said Taft. "And what is it I'm supposed to do for him? Besides pay him?"

"Not much. Just be there. Be with him. Get to know him a little. Get him to know you. Show him somebody's with him. Somebody's on his side."

"Somebody, meaning me? I'm not on his side."

"Then pretend," said Eli. "Act. Lie. Fake it. You can do that, can't you? Well, maybe not. Maybe you can't. Maybe you're too honest. If you don't have what it takes, well, then, forget it."

"I just told you I don't have what it takes, old top," said Taft. "Don't worry, though. I know where I can get it."

"I know you do," said Eli.

• • •

"The boy's a screwup," said Taft. "Eli likes him, but Eli's his cousin; he has to like him. In fact the boy's almost certain to be a complete mess. He's a criminal. He's born to hang. I've seen a million of them."

So have I, Chief," said Dangerfield.

"Eli thinks he needs a mentor," said Taft. "That's me. I'm to be his mentor, but lightly, invisibly. I'm paying him, but really I'm his guide, philosopher, and friend. He's not to know that, though. In any case, I don't want to be his friend. I don't think it will work."

Sure, it will work, said Dangerfield. *Look, Chief, you're not his friend. You're his confessor. You're his priest. A priest, is what you'll be.*

"Can you do that, old boy?" Taft asked. "Priests?"

Dangerfield laughed. *Nothing to it,* he said. *Priests are easy.*

"Ah," said Taft. "Of course, they would be."

• • •

Lucas's mother drove him by Taft's on Tuesday morning. She was late for work, but rather than simply drop Lucas at Taft's, she shut off her engine and turned in her seat to face her troubled son.

"You can do this, Luke," she told him.

"Yeah," said Lucas. "Maybe."

"Don't say maybe. You can do this, and it will be a new start for you. For us."

"Yeah," said Lucas. "Maybe."

"I wish you'd worn a clean shirt," said his mother.

"I'm painting a guy's house," said Lucas. "Why do I need a clean shirt?" His mom killed him.

"I'm so tired, Luke," his mother said. Then, "You can do this," she said again. She started the car. Lucas got out. He watched his mother drive off. She killed him. He turned to the house.

Taft had agreed for the job of scraping. "Okay," he had told Eli. "I'll sign the boy up for scraping, and I'll help him as I'm able. We'll get the place scraped and ready to paint. Then we'll see. Maybe I'll keep him on for the painting. Maybe not. As for the rest of it, the friend part, the on-his-side part, we'll see about that, too."

"Fair enough," Eli had said.

After his mother had left, Lucas waited on Taft's porch, at the front door. A big summer day, with big white clouds aloft moving fast before the wind but not much stirring on the ground, and the heat building up. Lucas was sweating. He didn't know what he was into here. He didn't know how to paint houses. He didn't want to paint houses. He didn't know what he wanted. He did know that he was at the end of some kind of road, or anyway he was at a fork. He knew more than that. He knew he needed not to fail. He knew that the hard surface he could feel behind him, pressing against his shoulder blades and his butt, was a wall. He thought maybe it was *the* wall.

No, he decided. Wall or no wall, he couldn't do it. He would walk home. His mother would be at work. He would get some things together. He would take off. He would hitch rides. He would get a job somewhere far away. A dangerous job, a job in a mine. He would die in a cave-in. But, wait: what if he never got that far? What if he hitched a ride with a psychopath, a murderer? What if he were killed, dismembered, his body never found, or even burned? No. Even that, Lucas thought, he could manage. Not this. Lucas turned from the door and started for the road.

Langdon Taft came around the corner of the house. "Lucas Polk?" he asked.

Lucas nodded.

"I'm Taft."

Lucas nodded again. He looked at Taft. He found he knew him." You were on the bus," he said.

"What bus?"

"The school bus. With Mandy and Candy and them."

"Ah," said Taft, "*that* bus." He said no more, but waited for Lucas.

"Um, I'm here about the—" began Lucas.

"I know why you're here," said Taft. "Come with me."

He led the way around to the side of the house. There he picked up a steel paint scraper, handed it to Lucas, nodded at the wall of the house, and said, "Have at it."

"What?"

"Have at it. Go to it. Any time."

"Um, I don't know if Mr. Adams told you," said Lucas. "I don't know much about this. Painting? I mean, I don't really know anything."

"There's nothing to know," said Taft. "This isn't painting, this is scraping. There are only two ways to do it: side-to-side and up-and-down. You can't go too far wrong. Come on."

They left the porch and went around the side of the house, where Taft took the scraper from Lucas and passed it across a section of the clapboard siding. Dry flakes of white paint flew in a shower from under the scraper. Taft handed the scraper back to Lucas. "You're off," he said. "See how you go. I'll look in later on." He turned and went into the house.

Lucas set to work. He scraped side-to-side, then he scraped up-and-down. Side-to-side seemed to go better, or maybe it was simply easier. He worked the scraper gingerly, tentatively, but even so, flakes and bits of paint filled the air, and Lucas saw he was making good headway. He began to feel easier. By the end of the morning he had scraped the side of the house from front to back to his own height.

At noon Taft came out and stood beside Lucas. Together they regarded the partly scraped wall, which now had a mangy, piebald look. Lucas waited.

Taft shook his head. "It won't do," he said. Lucas looked at the wall.

"Here," said Taft. He took the scraper from Lucas and stepped up to the wall. Bearing down firmly, he drew the blade along a clapboard that Lucas had scraped. More paint scattered behind the scraper.

"You didn't finish," said Taft.

Lucas looked at the wall. "You said there's nothing to it," he said.

"There isn't," said Taft. "It's one of those jobs, though. It's so easy, a baked potato could do it. But, God damn it, it still has to be done. And it has to be done right."

Lucas threw his paint scraper against the unfinished wall. "I'll have to do it all over," he said.

"That's right. Hell of a thing, isn't it?"

Lucas didn't reply.

"Courage," said Taft. "I'll give you a hand. I've got another scraper around here someplace. It goes better with two."

"You don't have to. I can get it."

"I know you can. I know you will. We'll both do it. For now, though, you must be dry. What about a lemonade? A Coke?"

Give him a beer. Dangerfield, in immaculate whites and wearing a jaunty straw boater with a purple silk band, was laying out the stakes and the wire wickets for a croquet pitch on the lawn beside the house. *The kid's been out here all morning*, said Dangerfield. *He needs a cold beer.*

"He's too young," said Taft.

Nonsense. He's had beer. Beer is why he's here.

"My point, exactly, wasn't it?"

Lucas looked at Taft. "What did you say?" he asked.

Careful, murmured Dangerfield.

• • •

By the end of the afternoon Tuesday, working side by side, they had the lower third of the north wall finished to Taft's satisfaction. They knocked off about four. Lucas walked home.

"How did you get on with Mr. Taft?" Lucas's mother asked him that evening.

"Okay, I guess," said Lucas.

"You guess. Come on. Did you like him?"

"I guess."

"What's he like?"

"I don't know," said Lucas. "He talks to himself."

"Your dad had him for a teacher."

"He did?"

"Yes. Your dad thought Mr. Taft was a fool."

"He did?"

"Yes," said Lucas's mother. "Of course, your dad thought everybody was a fool, everybody except himself. Look where that got him."

Wednesday morning, they were up on ladders, scraping away at about the level of the second-story windowsills. They had worked silently for the most part. Lucas didn't have a lot to say for himself. Those kids never do, especially the boys. They don't open up for you like a suitcase; they take time. But, for most of them, time is all they take. Taft knew that.

"Um, you know that day on the bus?" Lucas asked him.

"What about it?" said Taft.

"Well, about Mandy and Candy? What you did to them?"

"What did I do?"

"You turned them into, um, frogs," said Lucas. "How did you do that?"

"What makes you think I did?"

"I was there. I saw it."

"Don't believe everything you see."

"Not only me. The other kids saw it. I heard what they said."

"Don't believe everything you hear."

Lucas seemed to consider that. He drove his scraper along the wall. Silence.

"So, was it like a trick?" he asked Taft.

"Like a trick, yes."

Good, murmured Dangerfield. On the lawn, he addressed a croquet ball with a wooden mallet.

Silence from Lucas. Then, "My mom says you were a teacher. You taught at our school, she says."

"I used to," said Taft. "Long before your time."

"Did you quit?"

"'Retired,' we said."

"Why?"

"I was a lousy teacher."

"How come?"

"I didn't like the students. The students didn't like me."

"Me, either," said Lucas.

"Of course not," said Taft. "Of course they don't. You're not like them. You notice things. You think about things. They don't. You're different. You're exceptional."

Liar, whispered Dangerfield. *Tock,* sounded the croquet ball.

"I don't know," said Lucas.

"I do," said Taft. "You're not just another dumb kid. Anybody can see that."

Liar.

"Shut up," said Taft.

"What?" asked Lucas.

"You missed that spot, that spot over there, see?" said Taft.

They worked together without talking for a few minutes. Then Lucas asked Taft, "So, what did you teach?"

"Whatever they needed. History. English. Latin, when they had it."

"My mom says you taught my father."

"It's possible," said Taft. "What was his name?"

"Reginald. Reginald Polk."

"Sure, I remember him."

Liar. Dangerfield drove for position. *Tock*.

They worked on. They finished the north wall and moved around to the east. There, no longer on the weather side of the house, the work went more quickly. Lucas was pushing it, pushing the pace.

His father. Ask him about his father, Dangerfield muttered. He sent the wooden ball smartly at the wicket. *Tock*.

"What's your father doing now?" Taft asked Lucas.

"Um, he's gone," said Lucas.

"Gone, where?"

"My father?"

"Yes. Where is he?"

"Um, he doesn't live here."

"Yes. Where?"

"Um, Tennessee."

"That must be hard," said Taft. He made his scraper screech in a long pass over the wall. Dry paint cascaded down.

"What?" Lucas asked him.

"That he's not around."

"Hard for who?"

"For you."

Lucas shook his head. He shook his head and leaned into his scraper.

"It's not?" Taft asked him.

"No," said Lucas. "I don't care."

"Really? It sounds tough to me. Eli says you don't have any friends."

"Sure, I do. I did. I had a friend. Brian. But he moved away."

"Did he go to Tennessee, too?"

"I don't know where he went," said Lucas.

Dangerfield's ball missed the wicket by a foot and rolled to the edge of the lawn. He hurled the mallet after it. *Silly damned game*, he said.

• • •

Wednesday they finished the east side and started on the south. The south side was easy because it had an extra window on the first floor. By mid-afternoon they had it done and were ready to begin the west end, the gable, which would complete the job.

Something was eating at Lucas. He hadn't said a word all day. Taft waited. At last Lucas gave off scraping and, staring at the wall in front of him, said, "What you said yesterday?"

"What did I say?" Taft asked.

"About, um, Mr. Adams. What he said? It's none of his business, anyway."

"What he said about what?"

"About friends. The old fuck. Why's he think I don't have friends?"

"Because you don't?"

"What's it to him, anyway?"

"He's worried about you."

"He's stupid, then. If I'd wanted to kill myself, would I have crashed in a pond?"

"Who said you wanted to kill yourself?" Taft asked him.

"Everybody. My mom, Mr. Adams. The other kids. Everybody. That's what they think."

"Did you?"

"I just said. No. If I'd wanted to do that, I would have hit a tree or a bridge or something. Wouldn't I? Not a stupid pond. Wouldn't I?"

"Why did you, go into the pond, then?"

"I don't know. I don't remember much about it. I was drunk, and I don't remember. If you're drunk, you don't always remember. You wouldn't understand."

"Don't be too sure," said Taft.

Lucas resumed scraping. After a couple of minutes, he said, "He's in prison."

"Who?" asked Taft.

"My father. My father is in prison in Tennessee."

Taft nodded.

"You didn't know that?" asked Lucas.

"How would I?"

"Everybody else does. Don't you want to know what he did?"

Taft worked his scraper along a windowsill. He shrugged. "He didn't do anything to me."

"He killed somebody," said Lucas.

"That's tough"

"Tough? On who?"

"On whoever he killed, mostly, I guess," said Taft. "Also on your mother. On you. It's tough on everybody. But, see here: that's your father, not you. Right? You didn't kill anybody. Right? You're not in prison in Tennessee. Right? You're here, and you're free."

"So, what?"

"So, everything," said Taft.

• • •

Thursday afternoon. They were about done. Lucas was on the long ladder, near the top, scraping, scraping, working his way up under the peak of the roof. There's only room for one up there, so Taft, on the ground, held the ladder.

Above Lucas's head, Dangerfield sat on the roof, straddling the roof beam. Still in his croquet whites, now after three days become a little grubby, he was smoking a fat cigar, enjoying the fine late-summer weather, enjoying himself.

Look at him go, said Dangerfield. *This kid knows how to work.*

"He does," said Taft.

Are you going to hire him to stay on for the painting?

"I don't know. I don't know that he wants to stay."

Ask him.

"Lucas?" Taft called up the ladder.

"Yo," said Lucas.

"What do you think? We're about done. Do you want to come back next week, work on painting?"

"I don't mind," said Lucas.

What did I tell you?

"I wouldn't call that a ringing, vigorous assent," said Taft.

I would. That's exactly what I'd call it. Consider the source. He's a country boy. He's a Vermont country boy. What the devil do you want, Chief? Do you want it in blank verse?

"You may be right."

You know I'm right. I predict big things for this kid. This kid is going far.

Atop the ladder, Lucas let his scraper drop to the ground at Taft's feet. "That's it," he said. "It's done. Hey, how come you're always talking to yourself?"

Taft didn't answer. He let go the ladder and stepped back to let Lucas climb down. For that moment, the ladder was free. Taft turned, and started for the house. Just then,

Heads up! said Dangerfield, atop the roof, and he kicked the ladder away from the house. The ladder didn't fall, but Lucas lost his hold, cried out once, and came off the ladder backwards, his arms pinwheeling helplessly, like a doomed soldier shot as he mounts the wall of a besieged city—came off the top of the ladder, forty feet in the air, falling, falling.

Oops, said Dangerfield.

Taft was there. He caught Lucas in his arms the way you catch a sack of grain or coal. He didn't so much as waver as he took the boy's weight, but set him down lightly on his feet.

"I've got you," said Taft.

Lucas was shaking. He was white as a ghost. "How did you do that?" He asked Taft. "How did you get here? You were over there."

Taft winked at him.

• • •

In the study, Taft poured out a large Sir Walter Scott for Dangerfield and handed it across the desk. Then he poured one for himself. He sat. He faced Dangerfield.

"What was that for?" he asked.

What was what for, Chief? Dangerfield asked mildly.

"Kicking the ladder," said Taft. He was angry. "Throwing the kid off from way up there. He might have been killed."

Really, Chief? With you around? You watching over him? His protector? His friend? The moves you've got? The speed? The strength? Talk about Talents! I wasn't sure even I could put that over. But I did. That's our deal. As you may remember? So spare me the outrage, okay? Suffice to say, the kid was in no danger, and you and I both know it.

"Suppose he wasn't. Why do it? Just to scare him?"

Action, said Dangerfield. *A little business, you know, a little spectacle? Something going on? Something to look at? That kid? Sure, you're working with him out there, you're being his pal, his mentor, you're hanging out, you're shooting the shit. You're being firm, but kind; kind, but firm. Blah, blah, blah. And all that's okay, that's great—as far as it goes. But it was starting to run long, Chief. You know it was. It was starting to feel too much like Act Three.*

So I juiced things a little. It's all part of the service. Don't thank me.

"I wasn't about to thank you," said Taft.

Lighten up, Chief. Smile. Don't you get it? We're in show business, here. End of the day, it's vaudeville we're in. We are such stuff as dreams are made on, you know? You know that line? From your reading?

"I know that line," said Taft.

Sure, you do, said Dangerfield. *Show biz, all the way. What else? And so? Come on, Chief. You're the one who wanted drama, right? You're the one who wanted a plot. Can't say you haven't got one, can you? Look at you. You're up to your ass in plot—and you're the hero. What a deal, right?*

"Until the curtain comes down," said Taft. "Until Columbus Day. Or is that just part of the show, as well?"

No, Chief. On Columbus Day, the show's over. As you know, right? So what? My advice? Don't think about it. Have fun. Take the better, leave the bitter. Seize the day. Seize that sucker.

"You're a monument of originality, aren't you?"

In my line of work, you don't really need to be original. In fact, it can be a liability.

"Mmm," said Taft. "The bottle stands by you, I think, old sport." He nodded at the Sir Walter's on the desk between them.

Don't "old-sport" me, Chief, said Dangerfield. *I'm not your lumberjack chum.*

"My, my, old boy," said Taft. "Climb down. Bit tetchy today, aren't we? You yourself this minute said originality can be overdone."

Hah, said Dangerfield. *Okay, Chief, you win.*
"In any case, the bottle stands by you."
So it does, said Dangerfield, and he shoved it over.

9

A HELL OF A MARTINI

BOLD, HARD, WITH THE SWAGGER OF A LORD AND THE aggression of a fighting mastiff, the partner from the New York office strode into the dining room of the little country inn. Jack Raptor, the long-knife litigator, in town for the opening of court tomorrow. A pro, Raptor was, one of the victors, a winner whose suit cost more than a week's receipts from the establishment in which he found himself, and whose bonus at the end of last year might have bought the place—might have bought the whole fucking town, said Raptor, who, in his speech, affected the foul-mouthed dash of the rich and powerful.

He paused at the tiny, four-stool bar, but no bartender was visible. Raptor struck the bar sharply with the flat of his hand. A young man wearing a waiter's white apron appeared. "Can I help you, sir?" he asked.

"I don't know," said Raptor. "Is this a bar, or is it some kind of fucking church?"

The waiter smiled agreeably. "Sir?" he asked.

"Make me a white one," said Raptor.

The young man looked at him. "White wine, sir?" he asked. "We have a new Chardonnay—"

"A Martini," barked Raptor. "Beefeater's. Olive. Straight up. You know what I'm talking about? You heard of a Martini up here in the woods?"

"Oh," said the kid. "Yes, sir. One gin Martini. Will you want a table?"

"This is the dining room, isn't it? It says so on the door. Yeah, I'll want a table. I'm meeting somebody."

"He's here, sir," said the waiter.

Raptor looked. The dining room, brightly lit, had some dozen tables. This evening, most were idle. On one side of the room, two women were having their dessert. At another table, three men were being served. Near them, a family. At a table in the far end of the dining room, near the empty fireplace, a single man waited, presumably Raptor's dinner companion and coadjutor, the local hayseed lawyer who would appear in court with Raptor tomorrow and hold up the hometown end of the Shithead Posse as Raptor threw in the weight of the bank that retained him, united with the weight of his mighty firm, to crush, utterly, whatever poor fool had wandered into the path of his terrifying, annihilating onset. Tyler was the hick counsel's name. Something Tyler. Some hick name: Calvin or Virgil. Dumb woodchucks. Raptor turned from the bar and went to join him at his table.

"Do you want your drink, sir?" the kid behind the bar asked him. He was mixing the Martini.

"For Christ's sake," snarled Raptor. "No, I don't want it. That's why I ordered it. Yeah, I want it, okay? Bring it." He advanced across the room.

"Evening," said the man at the table when Raptor approached. "You're Mr. Raptor?"

"Tyler?" asked Raptor.

"Pliny couldn't make it."

"What the fuck? Couldn't make it? What do you mean, he couldn't make it. What the fuck is that?"

"He asked me to meet you in his place."

"And you are?"

"Adams. Eli Adams."

Eli, thought Raptor. There you go. Calvin. Virgil. Pliny. Eli. Fucking rednecks. Where do they all come from?

The kid from the bar brought Raptor's Martini and set it down in front of him. Raptor picked up the glass, drank half, devoured the olive, drank the other half, and handed the empty glass back to the waiter. "Again," he said.

"What can I get you, sir?" the waiter asked Eli Adams.

"Oh, I'll have a beer," said Eli.

"In beers, this evening, we have—" the waiter began.

"Anything at all," said Eli. The waiter left them.

"So, you'll be in court tomorrow, too?" Raptor asked Eli.

"I hope not," said Eli. "I hope nobody will."

"What are you talking about?"

"Orson Hayes. You're in court tomorrow about his situation, aren't you? You're going to try to get a judgment in his case, a disposition, or something? I'm not sure how you say it."

"You're not a lawyer?"

Eli shook his head.

"Let me help you, then," said Raptor. "We're not

going to depose Hayes tomorrow, we're not going to nego-
tiate with him, we're not going to counsel him. We're going
to foreclose his sorry ass."

"That's right. But, that was why I thought . . . I hoped.
You see, Orson? That's his home, that old place. He was
born in that house. It's all he's got. He's what? Eighty?
Eighty-five? He's not in the best shape. He's got a lot of
friends around here."

Raptor snorted. "Look, Virgil," he said. "Or, it's Eli,
right? Look, Eli. I'm sure what's-his-name's a good old guy,
but, you see, as far as I'm concerned, he's just another shithead."

"Shithead?" asked Eli.

"Deadbeat. Stiff. Bad debt. Nonperformer. Shithead.
If he wanted to hold onto his fucking house, he ought to
have seen that the fucking payments were made."

"They were."

Raptor chuckled. "I have a six-inch stack of paperwork in my case, up in my room in this dump, that says they
weren't."

"The papers are wrong. It's a mistake."

"Do I care? Do I fucking care? I just told you. I've got
the paperwork."

The young waiter came to serve Raptor's second drink
and take their orders. Raptor ordered a third Martini and
the loin of venison, very rare—"So rare," said Raptor. "So
rare, you can still hear the shot that killed the fucking deer,
get it?" Adams ordered the brook trout.

"Maybe I oughtn't to have said 'mistake,'" said Eli
after the waiter had left them. "Orson's place is out on Di-

amond Mountain. All that land, that's what Magog Partners has been buying up."

Raptor snickered. "Never heard of them," he said.

"You sure?" asked Eli. "We thought you would have."

"Who's we?"

"Me, and, mostly, the fellow who's advising Orson."

"He's full of shit."

"Tell him that."

"Don't worry. When I see him in court tomorrow, I'll be sure to tell him that."

"No need to wait till tomorrow," said Eli. He looked past Raptor's left shoulder and nodded.

Langdon Taft joined them at the table. He took a place beside Raptor, but it didn't look as though he'd come to dine. He moved his chair right up to Raptor's and turned it so he sat facing him, quite close. Too close for Raptor. He drew back a little. "Who's this?" he asked Eli.

"Langdon, this is Mr. Raptor, from New York City," said Eli mildly. "Langdon Taft. Mr. Raptor never heard of Magog," he told Taft.

"Is that right?" said Taft. "That strikes me as funny, though, since Magog's owned by the bank that's paying Mr. Raptor's ticket."

"Who told you that?" asked Raptor.

"I must have heard it on the radio," said Taft.

Raptor snickered again. "Can the radio prove it?" he asked.

"That might be difficult," said Taft, " seeing Magog is a corporation registered in Bermuda, which is owned by a fund in Zurich, which, technically, is what your bank owns.

Or it's what owns your bank. I'm not sure. Doesn't matter. And that's not even asking about the energy company in Dallas. Or the one in Russia. What's that one called? Ikon?"

Raptor moved his chair a little farther from Taft. He looked at him. "You've got a lot of bad info, friend," he said. "What do you want?"

"Mr. Raptor wonders what we want, Eli," said Taft. "We'd better tell him, don't you think?"

"We better had," said Eli.

"You want to fill Mr. Raptor in, Eli? You want to tell him about our proposition?"

"You'd better do it," said Eli.

"Proposition?" asked Raptor.

"That's right," said Taft. "A business proposition."

"I'm listening," said Raptor. "I asked you once. What do you want?"

"First," said Taft. "We want you to move on. Go back where you came from. Go tonight. Dinner's on us, of course. Then you check out and be on your way. You stand down on the Orson Hayes foreclosure."

"Stand down?" asked Raptor. "Are you out of your fucking mind? Stand down?"

Taft smiled at him. The waiter brought their orders. He laid the plates before Eli and Raptor. "Shall I set another place, sir?" he asked Eli, glancing at Taft.

"No need," said Eli.

Raptor handed his empty glass to the waiter. "Do it," he said. The waiter took his glass. "Enjoy your dinner," he said.

"Are you nuts?" Raptor asked Taft when the waiter

had gone. "I stand down? I go home? Don't be silly. I don't go home. You go home. You think you can just turn something like this off?"

"I can't," said Taft. "You can. That's our proposition."

Raptor shot him a crafty grin. "You're fucking crazy," he said. "But let's pretend you aren't. Even so, you haven't put out a proposition. You've put out half a proposition."

"That's correct," said Taft.

"Suppose," said Raptor. "Suppose I did *stand down*? I won't. I can't. But what would I get if I did?"

"It's not so much what you get if you do," said Taft. "It's what you get if you don't."

Raptor shook his head. Fucking boondockers. He was hungry. He picked up his knife and fork, cut a piece of venison, looked at it, and dropped his knife and fork onto his plate with a clank.

"I ordered rare," he said. He turned in his chair and snapped his fingers at the waiter, who was coming with his fresh Martini.

"I ordered rare," said Raptor again.

"Yes, sir," said the waiter. He put Raptor's drink on the table before him.

"So, you call this rare?" Raptor asked him.

The waiter looked at Raptor's plate. "Sir?" he asked.

Raptor pushed his plate away. "Take it back," he said. "It's fucking leather. Take it back to the kitchen. Send out the cook."

"Yes, sir, right away." The waiter picked up Raptor's plate and went toward the kitchen.

"And bring me another whitey," Raptor called after him.

"Fucking woodchucks," said Raptor. Eli and Taft were silent. "I ordered rare," said Raptor.

"Why don't you ease off?" Eli asked him. "You'll bust something. Eat your dinner. It looked alright to me."

"You don't understand, Eli," said Taft. "Mr. Raptor didn't get what he wanted. Did you, Mr. Raptor?"

"I did fucking not," said Raptor. "I wanted rare. That wasn't rare. I won't eat it."

"Mr. Raptor is dissatisfied, Eli," said Taft. "Maybe you should go and explain that to them in the kitchen. Tell the cook? Tell the cook Mr. Raptor wishes to see him."

Eli nodded. He pushed his chair back from their table, rose, and started toward the kitchen.

When Eli had gone, Raptor looked around the dining room. Then he looked at Taft. He blinked, looked harder. He was having a little trouble focusing his eyes. Taft had somehow grown dim. The room itself, which had been well-lighted, was now, Raptor saw, murky, and hung with shadows. It was also, suddenly, empty save for their table. The two women, the three men, the family, had left. They were alone.

"Hey," said Raptor. "Where is everybody?"

"They've gone home, Jack," said Taft. "It's not much of a late-night place, you see."

"Place is dead. Fucking woodchucks."

He's repetitious, whispered Dangerfield. He had joined them. He stood behind Taft's chair. He was got up in black tie, complete to the waistcoat, like the maître-d' in a restaurant far, far from where they were tonight. *He's repetitious. Like the other one. They're all repetitious.*

"You're repetitious, Jack," said Taft.

"Huh?" asked Raptor.

"Didn't care for your meat?" Raptor heard himself being asked. He looked up. Standing to his right, towering over him, was an enormous black man wearing a chef's white toque and tunic. He must have been near seven feet tall, and his skin, the color of strong coffee, glistened with sweat from the heat of the kitchen. He bent toward Raptor. He put the Martini Raptor had ordered before him.

"I said, didn't care for your meat?"

"Mr. Raptor," said Taft. "Say hello to BZ. BZ's the *chef de cuisine* here. BZ, Mr. Raptor. From New York. Oh, and this is Ash."

Raptor looked to his other side to find, standing near Taft's chair, another African, on the same scale as the cook.

"Ash is the sous-chef," said Taft.

Raptor swallowed. He attempted a smirk. "What is this," he managed to ask, "the NBA?"

"What's wrong with it?" asked BZ, the cook.

"With the NBA? Nothing," said Raptor.

"With your dinner."

"Um, I think I ordered the venison rare."

"No you didn't, either."

"Uh, I believe I did," said Raptor.

The cook laid a hand the size of a fielder's glove on the back of Raptor's chair and tilted the chair backward on its rear legs, then farther, as though he were a barber or a dentist getting ready to go to work on Raptor. "I don't care what you believe," said the cook.

The sous-chef, Ash, chuckled. "Don't nobody care," he said.

Raptor looked around the table. Now the room seemed almost dark, save for a kind of yellow light, candle light or lamplight, that played on their table seemingly from below. Taft and the two giants from the kitchen were lit obscurely, fitfully, as though by a campfire. Raptor gaped at them. How many drinks had he had?

"I might have had one too many Martinis," said Raptor.

"You might, at that," said Taft. "They have a special way of making them here. They're strong."

"Hee-hee," said BZ.

"Heh-heh," said Ash.

BZ let Raptor's chair tilt forward again. Raptor seemed to shiver. He chafed his hands together. "God, it's cold in here," he said. "It's fucking cold. Are the windows open? Can't they close the windows?"

Dangerfield had moved around the table to stand behind Raptor's chair, between BZ and Ash. *We're wasting time*, he whispered.

"We're wasting time," said Taft. "We need to wind this business up. Orson is in the clear. Paid up. Never wasn't paid up."

Raptor shook himself. He tried to clear his head. He tried to rally. "And I say he's in default," he told Taft. "I say he's in default, and I have the paperwork to prove it, like I told Calvin. Eli. Like I told Eli."

"Show me," said Taft.

"No can do, friend," said Raptor. "You're talking

about court documents. They're privileged, they're private. Besides, they're up in my room, in my case."

Beside Raptor's chair, Ash leaned over the table to hand Taft a leather portfolio. Taft opened it and took out a file of papers.

"Hold it," said Raptor. "How did you get that?"

How does he think? breathed Dangerfield.

Raptor reached his hand toward Taft. "Give that here," he said. But Taft was examining the file. He drew from it a paper and handed it across the table to Raptor. "This is what you're talking about?" he asked.

Raptor looked at the paper. "That's right," he said. "This is the bank's standard shithead letter to your deadbeat buddy what's-his-name?"

"Orson," said Taft. "The letter telling him he was behind, his loan was in default, foreclosure proceedings would commence, and so on."

"Right," said Raptor. "A shithead letter."

"It's wrong."

"You say. But do you know?"

"Yes."

"How?"

"Simple," said Taft. "I made the payments, myself. All of them, all on time. I made them for Orson."

Raptor curled his lip. "Very generous of you, I'm sure," he said. "But I have the papers, and the papers are what the court needs. They're all the court needs. What, do you think the papers are just going to disappear?"

Bingo, murmured Dangerfield.

"Hee-hee," said BZ.

"Heh-heh," said Ash.

"Exactly," said Taft.

"Oh?" said Raptor. "Okay. How? How is that supposed to happen?" For an instant, he felt the ground beneath his feet again—for an instant. For the last time.

"It happens when you put your papers, the whole file, into the fire," said Taft. He nodded toward the nearby fireplace. Earlier, it had been cold and vacant, but somebody had laid a fire, which now crackled briskly.

"Uh, why do I do that?" Raptor asked.

Tell him, rasped Dangerfield.

"Here's the thing," said Taft. "The papers are going into the fire. You don't decide about that. You decide whether you're going into the fire with them."

Raptor swallowed hard. He looked at the hearth, which was now a burning fiery furnace, blazing and popping, its flames licking up toward the mantel, its heat beating uncomfortably upon Raptor's flank. "That fire?" he asked.

Taft nodded. "You recall our proposition?" he asked. "You might say that's your performance incentive."

"That's some incentive, there," said Ash.

"Some incentive," said BZ. "Don't leave him on too long, though, Boss, will you?" he said to Taft. "He don't like his meat well done. Hee-hee."

"Heh-heh," said Ash.

BZ became angry. He yanked Raptor's chair back on its rear legs again, until Raptor was nearly horizontal. BZ bent over him and thrust his vast, shining face, like an ebony moon, into Raptor's. "Calling my *venaison du diable* leather," said BZ. "I ought to throw him on the fire this minute. You know what? I think I will."

"Oh, Jesus Christ!" wailed Raptor. "Oh, Sweet, Merciful Jesus, help me!"

Will somebody please shut him up? hissed Dangerfield.

• • •

Raptor raised his head from his arms, crossed on the table. He was drained, exhausted, ill. He looked toward the fireplace, where BZ was using the poker to break up the ashes of Raptor's documents. They had finished by throwing his leather portfolio into the fire along with its contents, and the air in the dining room was heavy with the smell of burning hide. In the corner the young waiter was putting the chairs on top of the tables. At the bar, Eli was settling their bill. The dining room was closing. Miserably, Raptor laid his head back down on his folded arms. Eli came back to their table. Raptor groaned.

"He's still drunk," said Eli.

"Kid mixes a hell of a Martini," said Taft.

A hell of a one, whispered Dangerfield.

"Mr. Raptor's got a long drive," said Taft. "Maybe a cup of coffee for him?" BZ started for the kitchen. Ash was no longer in the room. He had left them a few minutes earlier.

Eli looked at Raptor. "He's going back to New York tonight?" Eli asked Taft.

"Why not?"

"Well," said Eli. "But what's to stop him, when he gets back, from starting in on Orson all over again? He's got copies of the papers. He'll just come back after Orson, either himself or he'll send somebody else."

"What do you suggest, then?" Taft asked him. "Do away with him?"

Never a bad plan, sighed Dangerfield. *Can't go wrong.*

Taft ignored him. "What would you do?" he asked again.

"I don't know," said Eli.

"It will work out," said Taft. "We'll talk it over. We'll make our case."

BZ returned with a cup of coffee. He put it down in front of the collapsed and sodden Raptor.

"Mr. Raptor?" Taft addressed the lawyer. "Jack? Can you hear me, Jack?" Raptor hardly stirred.

"Yo!" snapped BZ at Raptor's side. He poked Raptor in the ribs. Raptor jerked awake in his chair, as though he'd been hit by an electric current.

"Don't hurt me," he pleaded.

"Relax, Jack," said Taft. "Have some coffee. Return to the land of the living. We need you awake. We need to talk. We need to reason together."

Raptor looked at the coffee but didn't touch it. "About what?" he said.

"About how you're going to miss court tomorrow," said Taft. "You're going to forfeit. You're going to drive back down to New York tonight, and tomorrow you're going to tell your boss to tell his boss to tell the fellows in Bermuda to tell the fellows in Zurich, and in Dallas, and in St. Petersburg, and wherever else they hide, to forget about this valley, forget about Orson Hayes, to let him off the hook, now and forever."

"And what happens to them if they won't forget about him?"

"To them? Nothing happens to them."

"To me?" Raptor said. "Look, I get it, okay, Mr. . . . ?"

"Taft."

"I get it, Taft," Raptor pleaded. "I understand. You've got nothing to worry about from me."

"I'm not worried, Jack," said Taft. "Not worried at all. Let me show you why."

Big Ash was with them again. He was standing to Raptor's right. Now he placed on the table, beside Raptor's coffee cup, a pair of gentleman's shoes, tasseled, highly polished, hand-lasted.

"Are these your shoes, Jack?" Taft asked Raptor.

"Yes."

"Did you pack them when you came up here for your court date?"

"No."

"Where were they?"

"In my closet," said Raptor. "In the dressing room in my duplex."

"Where's that, Jack?" asked Taft.

"Sutton Place."

"So, if you left these shoes on Sutton Place, how do they happen to be here now, do you think?"

"I don't know," said Raptor. "You do."

"Yes, I do, Jack," said Taft. "Ash, here. Ash got them for us. He popped down and picked them up, brought them back. He's quick, Ash. He can do that kind of thing any time he wants to. Go where he wants, do what he wants. Doors, windows, bars, locks, guards, cops—they're nothing for Ash. Have any trouble down in New York this time, did you, Ash?"

"Naw," said Ash.

"How did you like Sutton Place, Ash?" asked Taft.

"Real fine. 'Course, I've been before."

"And Mr. Raptor's duplex?"

"Fine, fine," said Ash.

"Nice view?"

"If you like Long Island City."

"Exactly," said Taft. "What else, Ash?"

"Man's got a lot of shoes," said Ash.

• • •

"God," said Taft, "look at you. Where in the world did you get an outfit like that?"

Dangerfield, seated by the window in a leather easy chair, smoothed the skirts of his dressing gown. The gown was of a rich, purple silk printed with large golden dragons, emerald-eyed.

Hong Kong, said Dangerfield.

"Hong Kong? Do you get out there often?"

As often as I can, said Dangerfield. *Now, that is my idea of a city. If you've got the money, you can get anything you want, do anything you want. Have you been?*

Taft shook his head.

Somehow, that doesn't surprise me, Chief, said Dangerfield. *Not quite your style, is it? But, sure, I go there quite a lot. Not as much as when the British were in charge, but still, several times a year. I told you, we're global. We're like Raptor and his people.*

"Mmm," said Taft. He chucked a handful of ice cubes into a glass on his desk and poured in after them a generous measure of Sir Walter Scott. He reached another glass and brought it toward him.

"You interested?" he asked.

Just a taste, said Dangerfield. Taft pushed the bottle and a glass across the desk toward him, then picked up his own glass and tasted his whiskey. He made a face. He leaned back in the chair and regarded Dangerfield for a moment with a speculative, morose expression. At last he smiled and shook his head.

You're thoughtful, Chief, said Dangerfield. *What is it?*

"Saw Orson yesterday," said Taft.

Yes?

"I went out there, I thought I'd tell him he's clear. He's safe. He won't be foreclosed on. Not ever. He doesn't have to worry, ever. The sun is shining again. Thought he'd be glad to hear it."

Was he?

"If he was, he had it under control. No, he wasn't glad. Not at all. In fact, He God-damned me up one side and son-of-a-bitched me down the other. What did I think he was, a charity case? Did I think he couldn't manage his own affairs? Who the hell did I think I was? And so on and so forth."

I could have told you. What did you expect, gratitude?

"I don't know," said Taft. "I guess not. But, some sign of pleasure? Of relief? I would have thought Orson would at least be happy he wasn't going to lose his home, for example. Hell, no, he wasn't happy. Fact is, he didn't know if he could stand another winter up here. He'd been thinking about selling the place and going to live with his daughter in Tucson."

Tucson?

"He's cold all the time, Orson said. Right from September, all through to May, he's cold. He said in Tucson they don't have that. In Tucson, it's always hot."

Hah, said Dangerfield. *If Tucson is his idea of heat, he's a child.*

10
SPLIT PEA

"**O**H, YES," SAID CALPURNIA. "I HEARD THAT."

It was Calpurnia's habit in conversation, Eli had long since observed, never to admit ignorance in any business concerning the valley or its people. Even of doings and actors that it was, as a practical matter, quite impossible she should have knowledge, she would let on to be informed. Had a space ship carrying a delegation from Alpha Centauri landed an hour ago on the town green? "I heard that," said Calpurnia. Was the new principal of the elementary school in reality the long-missing Russian Grand Duchess Anastasia? "I know." Had the same woman once played third base for the Red Sox? "Oh, yes," said Calpurnia. "Oh, yes."

No, Eli wasn't surprised that Calpurnia knew of the Polk boy's working at Taft's, or said she did. "That poor kid has never had a break," she said.

"He's got one now," said Eli. "He's painting at Langdon Taft's."

"I heard that," said Calpurnia. "Yes, well, it needed it.

I remember when that was the Jackson place. Judge Jackson kept it up like nothing you ever saw. Talk about paint? The painters practically lived there. Your friend has let it go."

"There you go again," said Eli. "'Your friend.' You keep on saying that. I've asked you why you're so down on Langdon."

"And I've told you," said Calpurnia blandly. "I'm not down on him. I don't know him, except for just around and about. He's polite enough, I suppose. Rides pretty high on his horse, though, doesn't he?"

"No, he doesn't. How does he?"

"Oh, ways. The way he talks. The way he goes around. I told you about his parents, what they were like. The apple don't fall far, you know. Even his name. *Langdon.* What kind of a name's Langdon?"

"What kind of a name's Calpurnia?"

"Calpurnia's somebody in a Shakespeare play. My mother loved Shakespeare."

"Why didn't she name you Shakespeare, then?"

"That would have been pretty peculiar, wouldn't it?"

"So's Calpurnia," said Eli.

"My, my, we're quick on the trigger today, aren't we?"

"I'm just saying."

"'Course, you stick up for him," said Calpurnia. "But you know as well as I do what he is. The bottle, and all."

"Langdon's mostly on the wagon, these days."

"Hah," said Calpurnia. "On the wagon, is it? It looks like to me if you have to have a special word for not being a drunk, you are one."

"Oh, is that right?"

"That is right," said Calpurnia. "You heard it here. Mind you, nobody wants a plaster saint. I never did. No teetotalers need apply. They're sneaky. A man should take a drink. There should be something he loves besides you. The thing is, with the bottle boys, they start by loving the bottle besides you, then they love it as much as you, then they love it more than you, then it's all they love, and you've got no show at all."

And you know this how, exactly? Eli thought but did not say, Calpurnia never having married, and being, as far as anyone then living knew, quite chaste.

"You men," she went on. "You never get set up just right, do you? If you're fond of the bottle, you aren't to be trusted. If you're not fond of the bottle, you aren't to be trusted. What are we girls to do?"

"You girls just have to roll the dice, it looks like," said Eli. "Guess and go."

The door of Calpurnia's room opened, and one of the Hospice workers stuck her head in. "Oh," she said, "I'm sorry. I didn't know you had a visitor."

"Come on in," said Eli. "We were just getting ready to start drinking in here. Plenty for you."

"Hush," said Calpurnia.

"Kitchen wants to know if split pea is okay for you for lunch," said the Hospice worker. "It's all they've got."

"That sounds fine, dear," said Calpurnia. "Thank you." The Hospice worker withdrew. "If it's all they've got, why ask?" said Calpurnia. "Still, she's a nice girl, that one."

"Cecelia," said Eli. "She's in that Polk family, too, somehow, isn't she?"

"Somehow, I guess. But really, that poor kid, that Lucas? What chance did he ever have? That family?"

"Sally's alright," said Eli.

"Sally *is* alright. I say nothing against Sally. She does the best she can. But her husband, her jailbird husband?"

"Reggie," said Eli.

"He never was any good. He went from bad to worse. It's hard on the boy. A boy takes after his father. A boy needs a father."

"I don't know if a boy needs Reggie for a father, though."

"Reggie's main trouble was he's lazy," said Calpurnia. "That's the heart of it. He got exactly what he deserved. He never wanted to work. Work? Not Reggie. He was too smart, he thought."

"It doesn't look like the boy took after Reggie that way, at least," said Eli. "It's not like he wouldn't work. He worked over McKinley's pretty good."

Calpurnia sniffed. "McKinley," she said. "Don't give me McKinley. That's the best thing about this, ask me. They ought to pin a ribbon on that boy." Her opinion of McKinley was known to Eli. It was known to everybody in the valley.

"That man is so tight he squeaks when he walks," said Calpurnia. "Pays the store help poverty. You want to buy a quart of milk, you find half the dairy case is gone by. Hardly heats the place in winter. Sells for cash only. Cash only? Whoever heard of a little country store that wouldn't let you run a bill? Years ago, when I worked there for Mr. Wilson? Two thirds of the customers were on the books. Tom Wilson didn't go broke."

"Yes, he did," said Eli. "That's why it's McKinley's now."

"Well, alright, I guess he did. Still, Emmett McKinley's a—I won't say it."

"I'll say it, then. He's a cheap bastard."

Calpurnia giggled. "No, really," she said. "'Course, Sally's boy oughtn't to have done what he did. You can't have that. But part of me's glad Lucas broke his window, the other stuff, wrecked that stuck-up wife of his's fancy car. Thinks she's so great. Good on Lucas Polk."

"Good on Lucas," said Eli.

"What's the boy going to do when he runs out of work at Jackson's, I mean your friend's?"

"Go back to school, I guess," said Eli. "It will be time. Sally worries about that, too. She says he hasn't any friends. The other kids are after him all the time, picking on him. Bullies. The worst of them went when Lud Grant left town, but there will be new ones. There always are. Teachers won't do anything—can't, maybe."

"That poor kid," said Calpurnia again. "School? I don't know. I sometimes think we were better off when I was a kid and nobody whose father wasn't rich even went to high school. You went to the common school until you were too big to get your knees under your desk, then they kicked you out and you picked up your shovel or your saw and you went to work. If you were a girl, you got married."

"Well," said Eli. "Langdon will help him, maybe. Give him someplace to go, anyway. Maybe Luke and Langdon will hit it off."

"I don't know if that would be such a good thing, though," said Calpurnia. "It's not just the bottle, is it?

Everybody knows your friend doesn't always have both oars in the water."

"They do, huh?"

"You know they do. I told you what Polly, at the Post Office, said about your friend's always talking to himself."

"You told me about what Polly told you about one time. One time ain't always."

"Well, it ain't never, either," said Calpurnia. "Polly saw what she saw. Could be it's something about the house, I suppose. Judge Jackson was mad as a hatter, himself."

"Besides," asked Eli. "What made Polly think Lang was talking to himself that time? Maybe there was somebody there she didn't see. Polly doesn't know everything."

"Polly might give you an argument about that," said Calpurnia. "But what are you saying? She was there, in the room, with your friend. He was alone. Was somebody hiding in the closet? Was somebody under the bed? Is that what you mean? Come on."

"I'm just saying, Polly doesn't see something doesn't mean nothing's there."

Calpurnia fixed Eli with an alert look. "Is that all?" she asked him.

"That's all."

"Are you sure?"

Eli was silent.

"Wait a minute, here," said Calpurnia. "Is something going on out there at your friend's?"

"Something, what?"

"Eli?"

"What are you talking about?"

"You tell me."

Eli shook his head.

"Eli?" said Calpurnia again.

The door to Calpurnia's room swung open, and a woman from the kitchen, one of the cooks, and not the Hospice worker who had been in earlier, entered with Calpurnia's lunch tray. At that, Eli rose to leave.

"Here you go," said the cook. "It's split pea today."

"I heard that," said Calpurnia.

11

THE MAID IS NOT DEAD, BUT SLEEPETH

ER FRIENDS TOOK JESSICA FROM THE RIVER AND LAID her out on the bank. Two ran for help toward the bridge, where several picknickers had seen the accident and were coming to meet them, delayed because they had to make their way over and around the river's rocks and boulders.

One of the two who stayed with Jessica, the Taylor boy, knelt over her and tried to revive her, but he didn't really know how. Soon he rose and stood, looking up, then down the river as though he were waiting for a taxi. Time passed. Minutes. Maybe five minutes.

One of the men from the bridge said he knew CPR. He went to work on Jessica while the others watched. More minutes. At last the man left off and sat on the bank beside Jessica. He lowered his head to his knees, breathing hard, sobbing.

Someone at the bridge must have had a phone, for shortly more people began to arrive. The first official was

Trooper Amy Madison of the Vermont State Police. She left her cruiser at the bridge and came up the river toward the group around Jessica. The stony, uneven riverbed didn't slow Trooper Madison. She ran over the ground like a deer, leaping from rock to rock. When she reached Jessica, she flung herself down and began immediately to perform vigorous resuscitation, but presently she too stopped. She shook her head.

"Nothing," said Trooper Madison. "She's gone."

By chance, Jessica had gone into the river near the spot where she and her friends had pitched their tent earlier. Trooper Madison directed that Jessica be placed in the tent. She and two of the others picked Jessica up and carried her to the tent. They bent and took her in. In the distance, approaching quickly, sounded the siren of an ambulance. Hearing it, seeing Jessica carried into the tent, the Truman girl, who had been with Jessica in the party, began to scream.

• • •

Jessica Kennedy: a famous kid, if regular kids can be famous. Well-known, well-loved. Jessica didn't have a boyfriend, but there wasn't a male in the valley over ten and under ninety who would not have plighted her his troth, if he could. Jessica would have been eighteen in the fall, was about to start her senior year at the district high school. She had thought about trying for college on an athletic scholarship. Jessica was a basketball player, light and not especially tall, but quick, stronger than she looked, and a leader. She also ran girls' cross-country.

With the confidence that comes from sport and successful competition, Jessica had also a daredevil streak, she had the kind of physical recklessness that is thought by some to belong, at her age, only to boys, but by no means does. As much as the boldest boy, Jessica would try anything. She had a flair for trouble—not real trouble, not bad trouble, but the kind of high-spirited trouble that good kids get into. Call it mischief.

It was Jessica who figured out that you could develop considerable speed going down the big ski jump in Brattleboro on your bottom if you sat on a plastic trash bag. When you got to the jump-off, you could bail out—or not.

It was Jessica who borrowed the line-man's pole-climbing spikes from the electric company's truck while the workers were at lunch and used them to climb to the top of one of the enormous old pine trees in the village. When the fellows came out of the café, there was Jessica, 125 feet in the air.

"Wow," said Jessica. "I can see Mount Snow."

When they demanded she come down immediately, she did. When they threatened to tell her father of her exploit, Jessica said, "Sure. What's he going to do, tell me I can't climb any trees for a month? Okay. I won't. I promise."

Who more likely than Jessica, then, to sign on to a whitewater paddle with four friends in a seam-sprung old canoe meant for two, with no life-preservers, no helmets, and no knowledge of or experience in surviving (let alone navigating) an enraged river in spate following three days of heavy rain? Jessica's contribution to the expedition's success was to observe that the canoe was pretty full and so to volunteer to be towed behind in an inner tube. The canoe went through a big, scary chute, with the others hanging on tight. Past it, they saw the people at the bridge waving and gesturing. They looked back. There was the tow rope. There was the tube, what was left of it. No Jessica.

Now she lay on the riverbank, unbreathing, near-naked, gray or blue in color, bruised, dripping, cold, and very still. A cruel, an unbearable business. Soon would have to begin the search for comfort, for strength, a search perfectly vain, reduced at best to reliance on ancient solace, the bleak assurance that the good die young and the young die good, spared as they are the disappointments, disabilities, and dissolutions that inevitably afflict those of us who live on. True, perhaps, but not a truth that has ever brought much relief to survivors in pain, or that could have done so in the valley at the death of Jessica Kennedy.

Except that Jessica didn't die. Not exactly.

• • •

Eli had happened to be at the clinic when the call came in for a drowning at the bridge. He rode on the ambulance. At the river bank, he found Taft just arrived and standing with the others.

"What are you doing here?" Eli asked him.

"Where is she?" asked Taft.

"I don't know. She must be in the tent."

"Let's go, then," said Taft.

There was no time. Eight or ten people had gathered around the tent on the riverbank. The younger ones held one another. Some wept. Others stood dumb and helpless.

Trooper Madison stood at the tent's entrance. She was trying to take a call on her radio, but she wasn't receiving well. "Say again?" she said. She listened.

Taft and Eli approached.

"Whoa," said Trooper Madison. "Are you her family?"

"No," said Eli. "We're here to help her."

"She's past helping," said the trooper. "We're waiting on the medical examiner. Please stand aside."

Trooper Madison's radio squawked again. She listened, but again she evidently couldn't understand the transmission. She left the tent and went down the bank toward the river, hoping for a better signal. When she did that, Taft stooped and went quickly into the tent. Eli followed him.

Inside the tent, Eli regarded the poor girl lying at their feet. She had lost the top of her bathing suit in the river, and, slender as she was and lying stretched on her back as she did, her small breasts lay like inverted saucers on her chest, juvenile, undefended. Eli looked away. He stepped to one side so Taft could approach the unmoving girl.

The Taylor boy was with Jessica, hugging his knees and rocking back and forth, not touching her. He wouldn't leave her side. Taft looked for some moments at the girl. He got down on one knee beside her and delicately cleared a strand of wet hair from her face. He picked up her left hand and held it in both his, chafing it gently. Jessica lay quite still. Taft put her hand back at her side. He looked up at Eli, at the Taylor boy.

"You'd better go, now," Taft told the boy.

Let him stay, whispered Dangerfield. He had come into the tent after the rest and stood in the shadow in a corner.

He wore a Navy frogman's rubber wetsuit, the glass face mask pushed up on his forehead, the broad rubber flippers on his feet slapping the ground as he walked.

From where he stood near the entrance of the tent, Eli watched as Taft laid his hand on the girl's forehead. "What's her name?" Taft asked the Taylor boy.

"Jessie," said the boy. "Jessica."

"Jessica?" Taft addressed the girl. "Jessica?"

Nothing.

"She's gone," said the boy. "She's dead."

She's not dead, muttered Dangerfield.

"She looks dead," said Taft.

"She *is* dead," cried the Taylor boy.

Want to bet? whispered Dangerfield. *Kiss her.*

"Oh, come on," said Taft.

"What?" asked the Taylor boy.

Go ahead.

Taft bent and kissed Jessica's forehead. He waited. Nothing.

Not there, murmured Dangerfield. *Dial it up a click, Chief. Go for PG-13.*

Taft bent to the girl again. "What are you doing?" Eli asked him. Taft kissed the girl lightly on the lips. He drew back.

Uno mas, said Dangerfield.

"What?" asked Taft.

One more time, Chief. Three's the charm.

Taft gave Jessica a third kiss. Eli started to speak again, but in that moment, Jessica stirred. She opened her eyes. She took a shallow breath. She sneezed. "Wow," said Jessica.

You lose.

"I didn't bet," said Taft.

Damnation, hissed Dangerfield.

Jessica blinked. She looked up at them. "Wow," she said again.

"Oh, my God," said the Taylor boy. "Jess?" he cried, "Jess? Oh, thank God. Thank the Lord. Jesus. Thank you, Jesus."

Get that kid out of here, ordered Dangerfield. *Jesus had nothing to do with this.*

• • •

Later, on the bridge, Taft and Dangerfield watched the departure of the car in which Jessica Kennedy, wrapped in several warm towels and surrounded by her jubilant friends, was being driven safely home. The ambulance had left. Eli had gone with it. The incident was over. Nearby, Trooper Madison was on the radio in her cruiser, calling in her report. Taft watched her intently.

"Did you see her?" he asked Dangerfield.

Who?

"Her," Taft nodded toward the trooper. "Isn't she something?"

You mean the skinny statie? Yeah, I saw her. She's the same one that hassled me the first day I got up here. Ballbreaker.

Taft hadn't taken his eyes off Trooper Madison. "She's beautiful," he said.

Dangerfield eyed him narrowly. *She's a cop, Chief*, he said. *Are you telling me you've got the hots for a cop? Don't be stupid. Listen, if you want that kind of action, I can put you together with people who'll make her look like a mud puddle. Just specify color and size.*

"No," said Taft. "You don't understand."

Oh, said Dangerfield. Oh, okay. Cops, is it? You say cops are your fancy? Cops in themselves? A little rough stuff? I wouldn't have thought that of you, Chief, but it's not a problem. Not at all. What's your pleasure? NYPD? Alabama Trooper? Texas Ranger? Gestapo? Name it.

But Taft seemed not to hear him. He continued to gaze at Trooper Madison. "Her," he said. "Only her."

Well, okay, Chief. Your call. The customer is always right. We live to serve. Do you want me to fix it for you?

"Can you?"

What do you think, Chief?

"But, how?" Taft pressed him. "She doesn't know me, not at all. She doesn't know I exist."

She will, said Dangerfield. *Don't worry. You want her, you got her. Fact is, this one won't be a heavy lift. Helen of Troy, she ain't.*

12

THE DIVING WOODCHUCK

"WHAT'S LIKE A WOODCHUCK?" ELI ASKED CALPUR-NIA. He took the chair by the bed, where she sat propped against pillows, her eyes closed. Eli regarded her. Calpurnia might have lost a little ground, he thought, the last few days. Her spirits were good, but she hadn't felt like getting out of bed. Eli waited. Calpurnia was silent. "What's like a woodchuck?" he asked again.

"What?" said Calpurnia. She opened her eyes. "Oh," she said, "what the doctor told Polly happened to the Kennedy girl. He was here, and Polly had stopped in, and we'd been talking about Jessie, and the doctor said there's a name for that. You drown, yes, but if the water's cold, it kind of shuts down your body so for a while you're like dead but not. You shut right down. Like a bear or a wood-chuck does in winter."

"It hibernates," said Eli.

"That's right. Instant hibernation, like, the doctor said. He had a name for it: diving reflex, sinking reflex. Some reflex."

"No," said Eli. "No way. That was no reflex. She was not hibernating. I was there. I've seen dead people. I saw her. She was gone."

"All I'm telling you is what Doctor Dish told Polly and me," said Calpurnia.

"Doctor Dish?"

"Doctor Dinesh. He's one of the doctors who comes in to check us all out, time to time. He's an Indian. Not our kind. An Indian from India. Nice man. Got his white coat. Little fellow. Looks to be about twelve. That's a thing about getting as old as I am, you know, one of the things: all the people you're supposed to listen to are babies."

"You listen to them, all the same, though, don't you?"

"Only when they tell me what I want to hear."

"So, what do you think? Do you think Doctor Whosis is right? She was hibernating?"

"Polly doesn't think so," said Calpurnia. "She thinks it was a miracle. She says their minister at that church they all go to—that Pastor Chet—told her later he'd been praying on her, on Jessie. But then Polly heard it wasn't so: the pastor was out of town when it happened. He and the vestry had gone down to Foxwoods on a package. He didn't even know about it till the next day. Polly doesn't care. She's with you. It was a miracle, you ask Polly."

Eli gave her a crafty smile. "Suppose it was," he said. "What's that make Langdon?"

"I don't know," said Calpurnia. "What does it?"

More than a drunk and a lunatic, like you say he is."

"I never said that."

"You said exactly that. More than once."

"Alright, then, suppose it was a miracle. Suppose your friend did it. What happened? You were there. What did he do?" asked Calpurnia.

"I don't quite know," said Eli. "But, I know this: the girl? She was gone. I saw what I saw."

"What did you see?"

"Nothing much, in a way," said Eli. "They had the girl in a tent she and her friends had put up. They were going to camp out, or they had camped the night before—I don't know. So Langdon and I go in there, and there she is, just lying there, and Charlie and Sue Taylor's middle boy— Doug? Dan?—is with her, very badly broken up. So Langdon gets down beside her and holds her hand and talks to her, and nothing happens, and the Taylor kid is carrying on, saying, 'She's gone, she's gone,' but Langdon must not think so, because he bends over and gives her a kiss."

"A kiss? One?"

"More than one."

"How many?"

"Three," said Eli. "He kisses her three times."

"On the lips, you mean?"

"Two times, it was, yes."

"You're sure about this?"

"I saw it," said Eli. "Sure, I'm sure."

Calpurnia was silent, narrowly watching Eli. Then, "The old goat," she said at last. "He ought to been ashamed. Taking advantage of an unconscious young girl? Disgraceful. What else did he do?"

"That was it," said Eli. "But that's what did the trick. The girl's eyes open, she starts breathing, talking. Basically, she's okay. Maybe a little pink on account of all these people looking at her and her having mainly nothing on."

"Hmm," said Calpurnia. She looked at Eli. "Was there anybody else there? When your friend did this?"

"The Taylor boy. I told you."

"Besides him?"

"Nobody I could see."

"Nobody you could see? What does that mean?"

Eli paused. Then he said, "Nothing." But Calpurnia wasn't having it.

"Eli?" she demanded.

"What?"

"You know what," said Calpurnia. "The other day, you were in here, you were so full of something you're about to bust. I asked, you shut up like a mousetrap: big mystery, big dark secret. That's enough of that, now. I don't like secrets. I want to know what's going on."

Eli hitched his chair closer to Calpurnia's bedside. He lowered his voice.

"See," he said, "Langdon has this idea, about how he did what he did for the girl. Not just that, either. About other things he's done, too. The money for Sean, more. There's a kind of deal, he says, an agreement, like a contract. It's pretty weird. Way he tells it . . ."

Calpurnia interrupted him. "Wait," she said. "Go close the door."

•   •   •

Eli sat back in his chair. He waited for Calpurnia, who said, "That is the craziest, worst, most utter stuff and nonsense I ever heard in my life."

There was a knock on the door, which opened to admit one of the Hospice workers.

"Your door's closed," the worker said. "Is everything okay?"

"Everything's fine, dear," said Calpurnia. "I'm sitting in here with a raving lunatic, but apart from that everything's fine."

The worker looked at Eli.

"It's alright, dear," said Calpurnia. "He's harmless. Go on ahead."

The worker withdrew and shut the door. When she had gone, Eli turned to Calpurnia.

"I told you it was weird," he said.

"Weird? It's beyond weird. It's . . . I don't know what it is. Who does your friend think he is? He didn't do anything, for goodness' sake. The girl was never dead in the first place. She was going to wake up. She woke up. Your friend was there. He was there kissing her, pawing her. That makes him a dirty old man. It doesn't make him a miracle worker."

"Spite of what Polly says, you mean?"

"Don't give me Polly," said Calpurnia. "Polly's a good, churchgoing, Christian woman. I don't begrudge her. Let her think what she wants. But she might believe a little too much. Polly gets down on the floor and commences to pray, and whatever happens next is a miracle."

"What would you call it, then, what happened there?"

"I'd call it good luck," said Calpurnia. "I'd call it what Dr. Dish called it. Diving woodchuck disease, or whatever it was."

"Pretty tough-minded today, ain't you?"

"I've seen things," said Calpurnia. "Things not so different. One time when I was little, these two boys from town—Tom Johnson and the other's name I forget—went out squirrel hunting on the hill behind the sawmill, there. They had one squirrel rifle between them. So of course it went off, and Tommy got it in the face. Went in right over his eye and came out the back of his head. Down he went. Well, the other boy ran to the mill for help, and the men there dropped everything and ran toward the woods. And, before they get halfway, here comes Tommy, walking down the hill to meet them. Got a little hole over his eye, got another around back. Little blood on his forehead—not much blood. Fit as a flea. Said his ears were ringing. Said he had a little headache. Soon went away. He was fine."

"You were there?" Eli asked her. "You saw it?"

"Sure. I saw Tommy. Everybody did."

"And nobody thought that was a miracle?"

"No," said Calpurnia. "They thought Tommy had a close call. He's a lucky kid, they thought. They didn't think anything more. Why would they? They had other things to think about. Like keeping body and soul together. Those being very hard times, you see. Miracles? It was enough of a miracle in those days if you could hang onto your little farm. So don't give me miracles. As for Tommy? Well, they were glad he was okay. Everybody liked Tommy. He delivered the mail in Bellows Falls for years and years. Lived to a ripe old age."

"Everything's a ripe old age after you've been shot through the head," said Eli.

"Gil Coolidge," said Calpurnia.

"Who's that?"

"Gil Coolidge. That was the other boy, who was with Tommy when he got shot. I couldn't recall earlier. Gil Coolidge. Gilbert. Trudy and Lee Coolidge's oldest."

Eli had to go. He got to his feet. He shoved his chair into the corner and made ready to leave. "Anything I can get for you right now?" he asked, but Calpurnia shook her head.

"Not right now," she said. "But, you know? I wouldn't mind if you'd bring your friend Mr. Taft around some time. Would you do that? I'd like to meet him."

"Even though he's cuckoo?"

"Even though."

"Good idea," said Eli. "You could get Dr. What's-his-name to have a look at him. Tell you why he's so peculiar."

"Doctor Dish. There wouldn't be any point. He's an old-folks' doctor, he's not a head doctor. Will you bring your friend?"

"I guess so. But why?"

"Well, fact is, the Kennedy girl is some kind of third cousin or great-great-grandniece or something to me."

"So's everybody else. So what?"

"So I'd like to see Mr. Taft. I'd like to thank him for what he did for the girl."

"But you don't think he did anything for her. You just said so. So why?"

"Are you going to bring him, or aren't you?"

"Sure," said Eli. "When?"

"Soon," said Calpurnia.

13

A THOUSAND SHIPS

TROOPER AMY MADISON WAS TWENTY-SEVEN. SHE WAS one of three women in the entire state to have been hired to do the job she had. She was bright, she was ambitious, she could outrun, outjump, outfight, outshoot, and probably outthink three quarters of her masculine counterparts—indeed, she was without detectible fault or flaw of any kind, or she wouldn't have reached the place she held.

That place, in a tough organization, a male organization, she had won and kept through decision, through action, not through analysis. She preferred to evaluate a situation quickly and react quickly. She preferred to be in motion. She didn't hesitate, therefore, when on patrol she passed a motorist stopped by the roadside. Seeing the vehicle and its operator, she immediately pulled over, reversed direction, and approached. It was a car she knew.

Trooper Madison drove past the strange car, a sporty two-seater, U-turned, and parked ten feet to its rear. She left her cruiser and came up on the roadster's left. This time, she was ready. At the driver's-side window, she put her hand on her service pistol and kept it there. The window opened.

Well, well, it's the Girl Scout, said the driver of the little car. He saw the trooper's hand on her weapon. *Whoa, Sweetheart,* he said. *Lighten up on the piece, okay? You're among friends.*

"Is everything alright, sir?" the trooper asked. "Out of fuel? Engine trouble? Lost?"

Heart attack.

"You're having a heart attack, sir?"

That's right, Sweetheart. I've got a little bit of a blockage going here, a little bit of an occlusion, a bit of the old plaque, you know? It's all the brandy and the béarnaise. Can't seem to stay away from them.

Trooper Madison looked the driver over. He didn't seem to be in any distress. He was the same stout, overdressed figure she had first seen along this same road some months before: same tweed jacket, same prissy cloth motoring cap. He smiled at her pleasantly.

"Are you in pain, sir?" she asked him.

Terrible.

"Do you want an ambulance, then? A medic?"

No need, said the driver. *You'll do fine, Sweetheart. I need you.*

"Yes, sir. I'll take you to the clinic."

No, said the driver.

•   •   •

Trooper Madison found herself in the passenger's seat of the stranger's car, driving carefully along an unpaved road through an autumn woodland: leaves brown, yellow, scarlet.

Where were they? Where was her cruiser? Where was her gun?

"Pull over, sir," she ordered. "Pull over, and stop your vehicle. Turn off your engine. Now."

Be cool, Sweetheart, said the driver. *We're almost there.*

"Where?"

Taft's.

"Why are we going there?"

A little business.

"You have business with Mr. Taft?" the trooper asked.

Not me, Sweetheart. You.

"I don't know Taft."

You will. Taft wants to make your acquaintance.

"So what?"

So, you'd do well to oblige him, Sweetheart. You'd do well not to get crossways of Taft. I could show you things . . .

"Sir, I say again: pull over."

Almost there, said the driver.

No, they weren't. Looking ahead, looking to the side, Trooper Madison saw the bright, particolored woods passing to their rear, but she felt no motion, and she saw no progress. She had the impression of riding in a car in a movie: the vehicle remains fixed while the scenery rolls backward in an unending loop of film, producing the illusion of forward movement.

The driver was talking to her. *I think you and my friend Taft would hit it off,* he said. *He wants to meet you. He's shy, though. But you'll like him. There's more to Taft than you might think. Oh, I know everybody says he's a lush, he's not playing with a full deck, all that. They don't know Taft. I could show you things . . .*

"How do you know him?"

He's a client.

"What kind of a client," asked the trooper. "Who are you? What do you do?"

Questions, questions, Sweetheart, said the driver. *Suffice to say, Taft's a man apart, a man to take account of. A man of talents. I could show you things . . .*

"What things?"

Things about Taft. About what kind of man he is. Have you ever been out East, Sweetheart?

"East? You mean like New York?"

No, Sweetheart. Capital-E East. Hong Kong.

• • •

Trooper Madison opened her eyes. She tried to clear her head. She found herself, no longer in the yellow woodland, but on the teeming street of a strange city, apparently an Asian city. The street was thronged, it was packed with people who flowed like a human river bearing on its flood cars, taxis, delivery vans, ambulances, scooters, and bicycles by the thousand. On both sides of the street, the stone facades of buildings like cliffs, blank and gray, office towers that soared into the invisible sky. In between them on the street were squeezed shops of every kind: tailor shops, jewelry shops, shoe shops, flower shops, noodle shops. The air was hot and dense, and a hot wind blew papers and other trash above the streaming traffic.

How do you like it, Sweetheart? Somehow, her driver had changed his costume. Now he was swathed in the flowing saffron robes of a Buddhist monk worn off his right shoulder and gathered over his left arm. His head was shaved, his feet, in white cotton socks, were sandaled. He gazed fondly over the chaotic hurry of the street before them.

This is my *idea of a city, right here*, he said, with a sweep of his arm that made his robe billow. *You can have your crummy country towns. Look at this, Sweetheart. Take it in. It's all here, and it's all for sale. Anything you want to have, anything you want to do, anything you want to be— it's here for you if you've got the price. Here, that's the only question: Can you pay down? Can you put the cash on the table? If you can, then here, you're free. You're free to be a winner. I love it.*

He drew Trooper Madison apart from the crush on the street and nodded across the pavement to the side of a building. *Of course*, he said, *there are winners, and there are also losers.* He pointed to a large cardboard shipping carton that had been shoved up against the granite wall of one of the towers. In its recesses, a dark heap of dirty newspapers and rags was visible. Lying on the pavement in front of the carton was a square of cardboard that had been crudely lettered

HOMELESS
PLEASE HELP

Beside this sign was a paper cup for change. The cup was empty.

Two men were standing in front of the carton. They were black, in their forties, expensively dressed. Both were large, well over six feet tall and massive in build. They peered into the carton, talking between themselves. One stooped to get a better look.

"He in there, alright," he said.

"I don't see him," said the other.

"Don't need to see him. You can smell him."

The second man bent to the carton and snuffed loudly.

"You right," he said. "Must be that guy from Goldman."

"Ain't nobody from no Goldman. That's Jack in there."

"Jack? Naw."

"Damn right, it is," said the first man. He struck the carton with his hand. "Yo, Jack!" he said. "Mister Raptor! Come on out of there, Jack. Say hello to your old friends."

No response from the packing carton.

"Ain't Jack in there, I told you," said the second man.

"It's Jack, alright. Look here." The first man bent, reached into the carton, and drew out a shoe, a tasseled patent leather loafer, at one time a costly piece of gentleman's foot attire, but now much scuffed and with its upper flapping off the sole.

"See there?" the man asked his friend.

"You right again. It *is* Jack. Hey, Jack! Wuzzup? How's everything down on Sutton Place, Jack? Hee-hee."

"Heh-heh," said the other man.

The carton stirred on the pavement as the filthy and abject creature within attempted, snail-like, to shrink farther into its shelter.

"How's it going, Jack?" asked the first man. "We were just talking about you, Jack. We were talking with Mr. Taft. You remember Mr. Taft, don't you, Jack? Up in the woods? 'Course you do. He asked after you, Jack. He's going to be in town next week, Mr. Taft is. Said he'd be glad to look you up, but he didn't know your, ah, new address. Now we can let him know where to find you. Be good to see Mr. Taft again, won't it, Jack?"

At that, a yellow liquid began to flow from the heap in the carton. It trickled out onto the sidewalk and ran toward the curb. The two men stepped nimbly out of the way of the stream.

"Look at that," said one.

"Man's pissed himself," said the other. "Disgusting."

"What's he afraid of?"

"Taft, it looks like."

"Taft? He ought to be afraid of us."

"He ought to be afraid of Mister D."

"Mister D, and us."

"And Taft. Taft carried the ball."

"So he did. Jack got crossways of Taft, and now look where he's at. Poor Jack. Another casualty of the Global Economy."

"Ain't got nothing to do with no Global Economy," said his partner. "Living in a box? Pissing himself? What it is: the man has no self-respect. That's what it is."

"That's what it is, alright."

"What it is, is a lack of self-respect."

"And getting crossways of Taft."

"And that."

"Amen."

"Amen."

With Trooper Madison and her guide watching them, the two men made ready to pass on. One pointed at the cup waiting for change before the carton.

"Throw him twenty, why don't you, brother?"

"Throw him twenty, yourself, you think so highly of him. Me, I never cared for the man."

The two moved on.

What did I tell you? Trooper Madison's guide asked her. *You saw that guy in the box. Don't get crossways of Taft. Cooperate. He likes you. You like him.*

"I don't even know him," the trooper protested.

Get to know him, Sweetheart.

• • •

Trooper Madison stood before the front door at Taft's. Nobody around. She looked at her cruiser, parked in the driveway. She was alone. She could leave. She ought to leave. She would leave. She would resign from the force. She would turn in her badge, her gun. She would move to another part of the country and find work in a library. She was leaving. She settled her belt around her hips, stepped up to the door, and raised her hand to knock.

The door opened and Taft stood before her. He smiled.

"Mr. Taft?" she asked. Right away, she felt foolish. Who else would he be? Taft nodded and kept on smiling at her.

"I'm Trooper Madison, Vermont State Police . . ." she began.

"I know who you are, officer," said Taft. "I've been waiting for you."

"You have? You knew I was coming?"

"I hoped you were," said Taft. He stepped back and let her enter the house.

Trooper Madison looked around her. They were in Taft's kitchen. She had been on the front porch. Then she had been at the door. Now she was in the kitchen. Taft fussed at the stove.

"Cup of tea?" Taft asked her.

Give her a drink, purred Dangerfield. In his most outlandish turnout to date, he appeared in the trappings of a ghetto pimp: full-length fur coat dyed pink; green three-piece suit, the open vest plunging to reveal a heavily pelted chest and a couple of pounds of gold chains and medallions lying on the fur; a diamond stud the size of a garden pea in his right nostril; a yellow broad-brimmed hat a yard wide, made of velour; combat boots, also yellow. He sat at his ease in the corner. *Give her a drink*, he whispered.

"A cup of tea would taste good," Trooper Madison said. "Thank you." Taft put the kettle on.

Slip a little cognac to it, whispered Dangerfield. *Get her loose.*

"How do you take it?" Taft asked the trooper.

She takes it any way she can get it, Chief. Like the rest of us.

"Shut up," said Taft.

"I didn't say anything," said Trooper Madison.

"What do you take in your tea?" asked Taft again.

"Sugar. And half-and-half if you have it. Do you have half-and-half?"

Half-and-half? Oh, Sweetheart, do we have half-and-half? Half-and-half is the way we have it best.

"Shut up," said Taft.

Dangerfield got to his feet and started on tiptoe for the kitchen door. *You're off and running, here, Chief*, he whispered to Taft. *Think you can manage on your own, now?*

"I hope so," said Taft.

"What?" asked Trooper Madison.

Tell her she smells nice, said Dangerfield. *They all like that.*

"Beat it," said Taft.

"What?" asked the trooper again.

I'm going. I'm going. Don't worry. Listen, leave a light on downstairs when you're, ah, all done, okay, Chief? So I'll know the coast is clear? I wouldn't want to interrupt anything. You know?

"That will do," said Taft. He crossed the kitchen and showed Dangerfield the door. Then he turned to Trooper Madison. He regarded her. He smiled and shook his head.

"What is it?" the trooper asked him.

"Here you are," said Taft. "Look at you."

• • •

So, Chief, how did you make out? asked Dangerfield.

"Is that your business?" Taft asked him.

I'd say it was, considering.

"I'd say it wasn't, considering."

Come on, Chief. How was it?

"You don't change, do you, old sport?" said Taft. "There was no It."

What happened, then? What did you do?

"We had a cup of tea. We talked. She left."

You talked. You talked? Listen, Chief, I can get the gun for you. I can load it. I can cock it. I can put it in your hand. But you have to pull the trigger. You wanted her, I went to work, you got her—and you talked? What was the matter with her?

"The matter? Nothing. Nothing at all. She's amazing. She's perfection."

She's too athletic for me, said Dangerfield. *Where's the tits, you know?*

But Taft was fond and far gone. "She's wonderful," he said. "We're going to the Fall Fair together."

The Fall Fair is it? Be still, my beating heart, Chief.

"We came to an understanding," said Taft.

An understanding? What's that do for you? Since when did understanding get anybody's pants off?

"Don't be vulgar," said Taft.

I'm not vulgar, said Dangerfield. *I'm frank. I'm candid. That's why I can bring up certain subjects—awkward subjects.*

"What subjects?" Taft asked him.

What subjects do you think, Chief? There's only one, at this point. It has to do with time. Look at the clock, Chief.

"Oh," said Taft.

Oh, is right. The clock is running, Chief. We need to have a conversation, don't we?

"Yes."

You're short time, Chief. You don't have forever, here. You know that? You're at the wire. We're looking at a date, here, now, you know? Columbus Day, right? That's what, day after tomorrow? We're going to have to close this thing. You want understanding? Understand that.

"I do," said Taft.

I hope so, said Dangerfield. *And by the way, Chief, something I've been meaning to bring up. When we close, last thing, I'll have my whole team with me.*

"Your team?"

The big guys, the stenographer, somebody from Legal, somebody from Security, the sketch artist, maybe a few more. It's a formality. But, point is, things can get busy at a closing. Hectic. People sometimes get emotional. People maybe say things they don't mean, you know? Suffice to say. So, before we get there, I just wanted to tell you, I've enjoyed doing business with you, Chief. I thought we hit it off—making allowances, of course. Different styles, and all.

"Of course."

I'll miss you, said Dangerfield. *So I will. I don't tell that to every account, either.*

"I'm sure you don't."

You don't have much to say, all of a sudden, Chief. Well, naturally you don't. I understand. End of the line, and all. We know it isn't easy. We have feelings, too.

"Of course you have."

But, the thing is, like it or not, a deal's a deal.

"A deal's a deal," said Taft.

So, said Dangerfield. *I guess that about does it. Like I say, it's been a pleasure. See you in church, Chief.*

"Well, well," said Taft, "but don't run off, old sport. Let's at least have a last Sir Walter's together."

He turned to the sideboard to reach the bottle, but when he turned back, Dangerfield was gone.

14

FRIENDS IN LOW PLACES

"**I** BROUGHT HIM," SAID ELI. "HERE HE IS."

Taft followed him into Calpurnia's room. From the bank of pillows that propped her up in the bed, Calpurnia held out her hand to Taft, and he took it, with a little bow. "Mrs. Lincoln," he said.

"Miss," said Calpurnia.

"Callie's still waiting for Mister Right," said Eli. Taft smiled.

"Hah," said Calpurnia. "Go ahead, sit, if you can find room. Try the chair." In the tiny room, with the bed, Calpurnia's armchair, a dresser, and a night table, there wasn't much extra space. Taft took the chair, and Eli sat on the foot of the bed.

"Cozy, ain't it?" said Calpurnia.

"How have you been?" Eli asked her. "Keeping busy?" He was watching her. Calpurnia's eyes seemed to Eli to have enlarged and lightened to a pale gray-blue. The skin of her forehead and scalp, the very bone, looked to Eli to be growing thin, like eggshell, to be becoming transparent. With that, though, she was much as ever. "Keeping busy?" he asked her.

"Awful busy," said Calpurnia. "Never a free minute." She looked at Taft. "That's a joke," she said. "I'm like the old fellow they tell about. Sometimes he sits and thinks, but mostly he just sits."

Calpurnia looked out the window. A tray from the clinic's cafeteria had been screwed down onto the sill outside. An overweight nuthatch picked and pecked among the sunflower seeds scattered over the surface of the tray.

"I sit here and I watch them," Calpurnia said. "The birds. They're pretty interesting. They're so feisty, especially the little ones. They're so crabby. This place must have a dozen feeders like this one. They put out fresh seed about every day. They have to. The little things, all they do is eat. And what, then? They fight, all the time, over the seeds. They chase everybody off. They're greedy. They're nasty, they're quarrelsome. And for why? That's what I wonder. Here are these tiny little creatures, they have all they can eat served up for them for free, they have their nests, their homes, everybody loves them, everybody admires them, they're beautiful, and if all that wasn't enough, they can fly. Anything they don't care for where they are, they can up and fly away to somewhere else. All that, and they're fighting? What for? What have they got to fight about? Why are they so angry? You're an educated man," she said to Taft. "Why is that?"

"They're birds, Miss," said Taft. "They're not philosophers."

"Like us," said Eli.

One of the Hospice workers looked in at the door. She

saw Eli sitting on Calpurnia's bed. "Can I bring in another chair for you?" she asked.

"You can if you can figure out where to put it," said Calpurnia. The volunteer looked again. She laughed. "Good point," she said. "Well, can I at least bring you some coffee?"

"That would be good," said Calpurnia. "But you don't have to fetch it. This boy can get it," she indicated Eli.

"I can?" asked Eli.

"Come on down to the kitchen, then," said the volunteer. "Don't hurry. They'll have to make a new pot, so it will take a little while." She left them.

"Go ahead down," Calpurnia said to Eli.

"You heard her," said Eli. "It's not ready. I'll go in a few minutes."

"Go now," said Calpurnia. Eli looked at her, looked at Taft. He got up off the bed.

"Close the door behind you," Calpurnia said.

When Taft and Calpurnia were alone, she smiled at him. She patted the bed at her side. "Sit here where I can see you," she directed. Taft sat on the edge of the bed.

"That's better," said Calpurnia. "I used to be able to see," she went on. "Had about perfect eyesight, never even needed glasses to read until I was seventy-some. Now it's as though I was wearing a veil all the time, couple of veils. Can't say I like it."

"No," said Taft.

"But, then. I don't have to like it, do I?"

"I guess not."

"There are some things, you don't have to like them, all you have to do is do them."

Taft smiled. "You sound like Eli," he said.

"It's not I who sounds like Eli," said Calpurnia. "It's Eli who sounds like me. I taught that boy everything he knows."

"I believe it."

"Eli's a good man," said Calpurnia.

"He certainly is."

"He comes here almost every day. He comes to visit me. He doesn't have to do that."

"He enjoys doing it," said Taft.

"I don't know," said Calpurnia. "I don't know if he does or if he doesn't. I know I wouldn't want him to stop. I don't know if I could do without him."

"I don't know if I could, either."

"He's a good friend," Calpurnia went on. "Friends . . ." she trailed off. Taft thought her mind might be wandering, but, "Everybody needs friends," she finished. "Don't you think?"

"I suppose so," said Taft.

"You suppose?"

"Well, if they're good friends."

Calpurnia shook her head. "Good, bad, either way," she said. "It doesn't matter. Friends is what matters. Having them. Can't have too many. Look at those birds."

"I thought you said all they do is fight."

"They do. They fight with their friends. Who else are you going to fight with?"

Taft smiled. "Eli told me you're hard to win an argument with," he said.

"We're not arguing," said Calpurnia. "We agree everybody needs friends. You more than most, maybe."

Taft raised his eyebrows at her. "I?" he asked.

"Oh, yes," said Calpurnia. She leaned forward in the bed. "I asked Eli to bring you around," she said, "on account of what you did for the Kennedy girl, that time. She's part of my family, and I wanted to thank you for what you did."

"I didn't do much of anything."

"You're too modest, Mr. Taft."

"Call me Lang."

"You're too modest, Lang," said Calpurnia. "You say you didn't do much of anything for Jessie Kennedy." She reached toward Taft and touched him lightly on the knee with her right forefinger. "I think you did," she said.

"No," said Taft. "It was one of those cases where somebody drowns but the water's cold, so they don't die right away. They can revive. That's what it was."

Calpurnia left her finger on his knee. "I heard all that," she said. "All that medical business. That Doctor Dish business. I don't believe that's all there was to it. I think there was more." She removed her hand and sat back among her pillows. She regarded Taft. "Fact is," she said, "I've kind of been keeping track of you, Mr. Taft."

"Lang," said Taft. "Why?"

"You interest me."

"Like the birds?" Taft smiled, but he was wary.

"More than the birds," said Calpurnia. "You know, there are people who think you're not in your right mind?"

Taft nodded.

"Polly Jefferson, from the P.O.? She's one. She says she came by your place one day, and she heard you inside talking and talking, talking away, talking to somebody who wasn't there."

"Oh, it's a habit of mine," said Taft easily. "I live alone. I talk to myself. I was talking to myself." But Calpurnia shook her head.

"No, you weren't," she said. "You were talking, but not to yourself."

Taft wasn't smiling now. "To whom, then?" he asked her.

"To an old friend of mine, I'm guessing. Well, say an old acquaintance."

"Who would that be?"

"That would be Mister Dangerfield."

Taft blinked. He became very still. "You know Dangerfield?" he asked.

"Oh, my goodness, yes. Mr. Dangerfield and I go back a long, long—a long way."

Taft was silent.

"And it's because I know him," Calpurnia went on, "and because I know who he is and what he does, that I'm guessing you need a friend—more than one, if possible. I'm guessing you have a problem, don't you?"

"Yes," said Taft.

"You have a contract."

"Yes."

"You have a date?"

"Yes."

"When?"

"Soon."

"When?"

"Columbus Day," said Taft.

"Mercy," said Calpurnia. "That's not much time. You could use some help, then, couldn't you?"

"What help?" Taft asked her. "If you know about this, then you know there is no help. I took his deal, didn't I? That's all there is to it."

"No," said Calpurnia. "There's more."

"What more?"

"Me," said Calpurnia.

"You?"

"That's right."

"What can you do?"

"I can go over Dangerfield's head. I can go upstairs."

"How? What have you got to do with Dangerfield?"

"As little as possible," said Calpurnia. "Put it this way," she went on: "Dangerfield and I? We're not on the same team—far from it—but in a manner of speaking, we're in the same game."

"I don't understand," said Taft.

"No reason you should," said Calpurnia. "No reason you have to. Dangerfield will understand, believe me."

"Why, though?" Taft asked her.

"Why, what?"

"Why would you help me?"

Lying back in the bed, Calpurnia sighed and closed her eyes. She passed her hand over them. She looked a little tired. "I told you," she said. "I've been keeping track of you. You interest me. You see, these contracts, like yours with Dangerfield? I've seen a good many of them. A good many. Ninety-nine times out of a hundred, the—what would you call him, the contracting party? Ninety-nine times out of a hundred, the contracting party wants the same things. First, he wants money, lots of money, so he can buy all kinds of stuff for himself and have fun. Then, he wants power, so he can boss everybody around and make them afraid of him. And, of course, he wants you-know-what: women, men, little girls, big girls, fat girls, thin girls, boys—all that department. Ninety-nine percent, that's what they're after when they sign the contract."

Taft watched her. Calpurnia's eyes had been closed as she spoke, but now she opened them and turned them on Taft. She beamed. "But you?" she went on, "you didn't want that, it didn't look like. You wanted to be of use. You wanted to be able to pay for that poor sick kid of Marcia's. You wanted that moron of a wife-beater to disappear. You wanted the Polk boy to have a break, you stuck up for him with those kids who were making his life so miserable. Then you took him in and gave him something to do and a reason to do it when his next stop was jail or worse. You put the boots to the bank's fancy lawyer when he came to kick that old fool Orson Hayes off his place. You brought Jessie back from the other side. You didn't do any of that for yourself. Far as I can tell, you didn't want anything."

"Well," said Taft. "There was one thing."

"Hah," said Calpurnia. "You're talking about that little policewoman. Well, I wasn't counting her. She's a little slip of a girl, is all."

"She's a state trooper," said Taft with a smile. "Can there be a little slip of a state trooper?"

"I have nothing against her," said Calpurnia. "But I

said she's a little slip of a girl, and that's what she is. Just because she wears a gun and can do a thousand push-ups, doesn't make her anything else. You're welcome to her."

Taft gave Calpurnia a long, thoughtful look, but then he shook his head. "What makes you think you can do anything?" he asked. "What makes you think you can do anything with Dangerfield?"

"Not with him. His boss."

"You know his boss, too?"

"I know them all, Mr. Taft," said Calpurnia. "And they all know me."

"Lang," said Taft again. "Friends in high places, eh?"

"No, Lang," said Calpurnia. "Not high places. Low places. Way down low."

"Suppose you're right," said Taft. "What can you do with Dangerfield's boss?"

"I've got a deal for him."

"What deal?"

"Never mind what deal."

"What if he doesn't like your deal?"

"He'll like it."

There was a bump on the door of the room. It swung open, and Eli came awkwardly through it carrying a tray with three cups, a sugar bowl, and a carton of milk.

"Coffee's up," said Eli.

15

THE DEVIL IN THE VALLEY

DANGERFIELD'S SUPERIOR, THE LEADER, THE PRINCE, THE big man, the big bug—pick a name, pick a title—arrived in the valley in the deepest, darkest middle of the night. He went straight to the clinic, where he entered through the Emergency Room. Night staff was on duty there, but nobody saw the leader as he went to the corridor where the Hospice was. On that corridor, everybody was fast asleep and had been for hours—everybody except Calpurnia Lincoln. The leader knocked softly on her door and went in.

"Well, well," said Calpurnia, "late, as usual." She was sitting up in bed, waiting for him.

Calpurnia, said the visitor, *lovely, as usual.*

"You're a liar," said Calpurnia.

They say.

"Take the chair," said Calpurnia.

I'll stand. Can't stay. Must fly.

"Heavy night?"

They're all heavy.

"Poor you," said Calpurnia. "You work too hard."

Leave the cheap sarcasm, Callie, said the other. *We both know you work as hard as I do.*

"I enjoy my work."

And I don't? Well, well, we won't bandy words. You wanted to meet. Here I am. I understand old Danger's account is being difficult.

"He's reluctant."

They're all reluctant, Callie. At the gate, they're eager, but at the finish line, they're all reluctant.

"Funny about that, isn't it?" said Calpurnia. "But this one? This one's not for you. Let him go. Write him off. He'd never catch on. He's different. Read his file."

I have read it. I know what you're saying. But so what? Look, this guy got his end, didn't he? He got the money. He got the moves. Everything. The Talents? He got them. He used them. He had a fine time. He got to be everybody's benefactor, everybody's protector. And then, his reward? He got that skinny cop. Got her on a silver platter with an apple in her mouth. Danger made it happen on our end. He always does. Danger's the best—not that I'd tell him that. But, now? Now it's time to pay up. A deal's a deal.

"Not if it's one of your deals, it isn't."

Her visitor smiled. *Touché, Callie,* he said. *I'm not sure I understand, though. What's your interest?*

"My interest is my business. Never mind my interest."

Why am I here, then? You want me to let your guy off the hook? Out of the goodness of my heart? Sorry, not happening. So why else am I here?

"I have an offer for you."

An offer? Okay, I know what you want. What is it you're offering?

"Me. I'm offering myself. I take myself out."

The leader approached her bed. He sat lightly down at the foot. For a moment he didn't say anything. Then,

You go away? he asked.

Calpurnia nodded.

Vacation?

"More. Call it a sabbatical."

How long?

"Long enough."

How long? Forever?

"*Forever?*" Calpurnia mocked him. "Did you say forever? You must be getting old. Forever? You know better than that. I said long enough. I'm out for as long as I'm out. What do you care how long? However long it is or isn't, are you going to get a better offer?"

Hmm. You for this rummy Eagle Scout? I'm tempted, I'll admit that.

"*You?*" said Calpurnia. "*You're* tempted? That's a good one." But her visitor let it go by.

I'm tempted, he went on, *but I'm also puzzled. You're pretty far out front on this one. You're going all-in for this guy. And frankly, when I look at him, I don't see the worth. Taking your point of view, I mean.*

"You cannot possibly take, or even imagine, my point of view," said Calpurnia.

Maybe not, but answer the question. What's he got?

"If you have to ask, then there's no answer."

Back to that, are we? said her guest. He sighed. *Suit*

yourself, Callie. We won't argue. I could call you a senti-mental fool—for the ten-millionth time. But I won't.

"Thank you for that, at least," said Calpurnia.

Danger will be unhappy. I'll hear about it from Danger.

"Dangerfield's your problem," said Calpurnia. "Give him a raise. Put new carpet in his office. You'll think of something. You always do. You'll take it, then?"

The visitor smiled at her. He patted the bed cover over her ankles. *I'll take it. Sure, I'll take it. You knew I would. How could I not?* He leaned toward her on the bed. His eyes were bright. *You know, Callie, I'm very fond of you. More than fond. I'm attracted. Very attracted. I'm sure you've seen it. I know I shouldn't be. But all these years? Years and years? We should be better friends.*

"Never," said Calpurnia.

Don't be small, Callie. Don't be unimaginative. Here are you, here am I. Quite alone. Past midnight. In your bed-room. What are we waiting for? We don't have to play by the rules. There are no rules. What do you say?

"I say you have some nerve."

Nerve? said her visitor. *Have I? Well, of course I have. Of course I have nerve, Callie, darling. None but the brave deserve the fair.*

"You and your fancy nonsense. Who do you think you're dealing with? What do you take me for, one of your milkmaids?"

Ah, Callie, Callie. Be nice.

"Buzz off," said Calpurnia.

• • •

The next morning first thing, when Cecelia, the Hospice worker, rapped on Calpurnia's door with her breakfast, she knew immediately what she would find. All she could say later was that the door didn't sound the same. The door sounded different, and Cecelia knew why. That's all she knew, and that's all she could say. She opened the door and went in. There was Calpurnia. Cecelia brought her breakfast tray back to the nurses' station. She called Eli Adams.

• • •

From the first minutes, Dangerfield knew what the play was. Secretly, he felt relief. He'd been down this street before. Still, he'd make the business yield whatever it might be worth to him. *I know what this is, you know*, he said.

What is it? his superior asked him.

The four of them were in the bar at the inn, the same ground from which the unfortunate Jack Raptor had advanced to his undoing. The bar was closed, so was the dining room. The inn was empty. Dangerfield's boss sat to his left, big Ash to his right. BZ was behind the bar.

What is it? the boss asked.

I'm being pulled, said Dangerfield.

Reassigned.

Pulled, God damn it, said Dangerfield. *My guy is being cut loose. All the development I put in, all the grooming, months and months, a whole summer—up the flue. And why? To please fucking Calpurnia. Calpurnia gives you a half-second peek down the front of her dress. And I get pulled.*

Reassigned, said Dangerfield's superior.

Well, God damn it to hell, said Dangerfield.

"Hee-hee," said BZ.

"Heh-heh," said Ash.

Another round, said the leader. *On me.*

It better be on you, said Dangerfield. *Letting that old bitch take the lead out of your pencil. What are you trying to do, here, win the popularity prize? You can't run a thing like this by being agreeable. You used to understand that.*

I understand it now, said the boss. *It's you who doesn't understand. This is not a schoolyard. This is not a matter of the lead in my pencil, or yours. It's a simple trade, that's all. It's business. It's about value. That old bitch, as you're pleased to call her, has high value. Very high. To take her off the court, even for a couple of games? Well, for that I'd trade a lot. I'd pull a lot of people. Would I trade a potted plant like your boy Taft? Of course I would, as soon as snap my fingers. I wouldn't hesitate. I'd even pull you.*

"Hee-hee," said BZ

"Heh-heh," said Ash.

You'll regret it, said Dangerfield.

Danger, I sit here listening to you piss and moan, and I regret it already, said the leader. *Not really. Has to be done. Don't worry, though, you'll like the outcome. I told you, you're reassigned.*

Uh-huh, said Dangerfield. *Where to?*

You're being rotated through the Home Office.

You're kidding, right? said Dangerfield. *Tell me you're kidding.*

The leader shook his head.

I'm no good in the Home Office, said Dangerfield. *I'm a field man.*

That's why you're going to the Home Office.

Balls, said Dangerfield. But his superior went on.

It's the young people, he said. *The young people coming up? The trainees? We're not seeing everything we need to see in them. They've got the technical side down, the engineering, sure. They're bright. They're entrepreneurial. But they can't sell. They can't close. They don't have the people skills. They can't relate. It comes to this: they're not having fun, and it shows.*

I can't teach them to have fun, said Dangerfield. *Nobody can.*

You don't teach them, Danger, you show them.

God damn it, said Dangerfield. *I won't go. You can't ask me to go.*

I'm not asking, said his superior.

"Hee-hee," said BZ.

"Heh-heh," said Ash.

You've got your orders, then, said Dangerfield's boss. *Look, you'll be fine. I told you: it's a rotation. It's temporary.*

Temporary? asked Dangerfield. *You're telling me it's temporary?*

Well, well, said his superior.

I'll say one thing. I won't be sorry to get out of here, said Dangerfield. *I've been stuck in this God-damned valley long enough. I've had it up to here with these woodchucks. They aren't businesslike. They want it both ways.*

Doesn't everybody?

To hell with the lot of them, said Dangerfield.

We're working on it, said his superior.

EPILOGUE
LARGELY ATTENDED

COUPLE OF HUNDRED PEOPLE WERE AT THE CHURCH FOR Calpurnia's service. They filled the pews, they stood up and down the aisles, they stood around outside, on the steps, on the grass. Then, fifty or more must have come along to the cemetery, on the hill above the village. There they stood at the grave and listened to the minister.

Polly Jefferson was at the rear of the gathering. She looked about her. A fine October morning: bright, the air clear, tuned, ready to ring like struck crystal, the trees turning color, and the many hydrangeas planted here and there around the cemetery in full display.

"Lincoln Services Largely Attended." Polly was the local correspondent for the Brattleboro newspaper. Later today she would have to compose and file Calpurnia's funeral notice, and she was assembling her thoughts. Largely attended was right enough. Polly couldn't recall seeing this many at a graveside. Not surprising, given Calpurnia's being the great-great-somebody-or-other of the whole valley; but still, a good turnout. Polly knew what Calpurnia herself would say about it. Calpurnia would make one of her sharp remarks, something like, why wouldn't people come? The eats are free, the coffee's hot, and the guest of honor won't be making a speech. Something designed to show how tough she was, how hardened, how unfeeling, all things Polly knew Calpurnia absolutely was not. Well, tough, maybe, to last as long as she had. Ninety-eight was no joke.

Polly reminded herself to be sure she had the minister's name right: Harrison, was it, or Harrington? She would ask Dorothea Clinton. Dorothea was the oldest of Calpurnia's nieces. She had left the valley when she married, lived in St. Johnsbury. In the couple of days after Calpurnia's death, Dorothea had swept in and pretty much taken over the arrangements. She had brought in her minister from upstate to perform the service. Polly would have liked her own Pastor Chet to do that, but Dorothea was a high Episcopalian and wouldn't have stood for it. And, in fact, Calpurnia had had no opinion of Pastor Chet, either.

The truth was, Calpurnia had not been a believer. Let people believe whatever they like, Calpurnia said, which to Polly was no different from her being an atheist. Not that they argued about it. What would have been the point? They were friends. Polly knew Calpurnia didn't believe. But she knew more: she knew Jesus knew it, too, and she knew He didn't care. He loved Calpurnia anyway, exactly as He loved Polly, exactly as He loved everybody. If Calpurnia's unbelief didn't matter to Jesus, why should it matter to Polly? It shouldn't, it didn't. And anyway, as Polly stood in the cemetery with the rest, she knew—she knew for certain sure—

that if Calpurnia hadn't been a believer in life, she was a believer now.

At the head of the grave, Dorothea's imported priest, in his gown and dog collar, was winding things up. Polly tried to move a little closer. She listened intently. Much as she missed having Pastor Chet here, she was moved, she was somehow satisfied, by the words of the old service, which the minister now pronounced:

> Unto God's gracious mercy and protection we commit you. The Lord bless you and keep you. The Lord make his face to shine upon you, and be gracious unto you. The Lord lift up his countenance upon you, and give you peace, both now and evermore. *Amen.*

Amen. People began to turn, to break up, to move. Now Polly could see Eli Adams standing toward the front, near the grave. Beside him was his friend Langdon Taft. Polly gave Taft a good look over. He appeared sane and sober, and he was dressed up in a jacket and tie; but she didn't plan on speaking to him. Then she saw the little State Police girl standing beside Taft, close beside. Hmm, said Polly, what's this? If the trooper girl was getting mixed up with Taft, somebody ought to have a friendly word with her. Polly liked the trooper. She had been as nice as she could be the time Polly called the State Police when her cat went missing. The trooper had come to her house and helped her look. Turned out the cat had gone down cellar for reasons of her own. They found her right off. She hadn't been lost at all. But the trooper had been as nice as she could be about the whole silly business.

The trooper was in uniform. Polly stood on her tiptoes to try and see if she was wearing her gun. She had been when she came about the cat. Polly hoped she wasn't today. She hoped the trooper wasn't wearing a gun practically in church. Though Pastor Chet said there were congregations out west, down south, where worshippers did wear their guns in church. In fact, they were expected to. Calpurnia would have had something to say about that, too.

Eli, Taft, and Trooper Madison had left the grave and were moving down the hill to where people had parked their vehicles along the road that went by the cemetery. Polly followed them. She examined the trooper's midsection from behind. No gun. She caught up with the three of them. Polly put herself as far as she could get from Taft, next to Eli, who, of course, had been closer to Calpurnia than anybody.

"How are you doing?" she asked him.

"I'm doing alright, Polly," said Eli. "How about you?"

"Well, you know," said Polly. "But I thought everything went off very well. Dora should be pleased."

"Yes," said Eli.

"'Course," said Polly, "Callie wasn't a churchgoer."

"No," said Eli.

"Not that it matters," said Polly.

"Not that it does."

"The point is," said Polly, "she's in a better place."

"She didn't want a better place," said Eli.

"No," said Taft. "That's right. She didn't."

"I don't think I ever met her," said Amy Madison.

"She was a good old girl," said Eli.

"One in a million," said Taft.

"We'll miss her, for sure," said Polly. "You know, it's hard to believe she's really gone forever."

She hadn't been speaking to Taft, but it was Taft who turned to her with what Polly thought was an odd little smile, and said,

"Very hard."